Laura t...
the conquering Moor

Thirteen hundred years before, Tarik ibn Ziad had invaded Gibraltar, claiming it as his own.

But instead of the image of the bearded Moor, Laura's mind was filled with the stern features of Brent Lewis, his piercing brown eyes agleam with mockery, his mouth curved in an ironic twist.

Laura suddenly felt very warm, and she lifted the heavy fall of her hair from her neck. Brent was no threat, no aggressive invader. He was here simply to do a job.

But, an inner voice reminded her, it was a job in which she was deeply, intimately involved.

Laura shivered.

Dana James lives with her husband and three children in a converted barn on the edge of a Cornish village. She has written thrillers, historical romances and doctor-nurse romances but is now concentrating her efforts on writing contemporary romance fiction. In addition to extensive researching, which she adores, the author tries to write for at least four hours every day.

Books by Dana James

HARLEQUIN ROMANCE

2632—DESERT FLOWER
2841—THE MARATI LEGACY
2872—THE EAGLE AND THE SON

Tarik's Mountain

Dana James

Harlequin Books

TORONTO • NEW YORK • LONDON
AMSTERDAM • PARIS • SYDNEY • HAMBURG
STOCKHOLM • ATHENS • TOKYO • MILAN

Original hardcover edition published in 1988
by Mills & Boon Limited

ISBN 0-373-02926-8

Harlequin Romance first edition August 1988

CHAPTER ONE

LAURA lifted the borrowed typewriter on to the long reception desk. Behind it, some distance away, the girl and the young man both smiled politely but made no move to come forward, knowing it was Inez she wanted. Leaning forward, Laura called through the open door into the office beyond. 'Inez?'

The sleek, dark head of the chief receptionist appeared, her round face breaking at once into a smile. 'You have finished already?' Neither a severe hairstyle nor crisp white blouse and plain navy skirt could disguise the warmth of personality and bubbling good humour Inez exuded.

On her arrival in Gibraltar two months previously Laura had realised within minutes of their meeting that Inez was one of this prestigious hotel's greatest assets. She nodded, her own pleasure magnified by Inez's unfeigned delight.

'Where will you sell the article? To *Wildlife Magazine* again?'

Raising crossed fingers Laura nodded once more. 'I hope so. They said they would like to see anything else I did.'

'I think it's wonderful.' Inez spread her hands, sounding ever more Spanish in her excitement. 'I think soon the managing director of Phoenix Development must find a new personal assistant. You will become a writer instead.'

Laughing, Laura shook her head, and her tawny hair tumbled wildly about her shoulders. 'I would soon starve.' She looked down, viewing her sandals, pale blue cotton jeans and matching fisherman's sweater with a rueful expression. 'I must admit, though, I hardly look the executive type.'

Inez tossed her head impatiently. 'This is your first day off in nearly two weeks. Today you are a writer, and writers can dress as they please.'

'You're so good for me, Inez,' Laura smiled. 'You always say exactly the right thing. But I'm not ready to give up my job yet. Despite my occasional moan, I really do enjoy it.' Her voice faltered and her smile faded. 'I went through rather a lot to get it, and even more to keep it.' She caught herself, and with determined brightness went on, 'Besides, I'm very happy living here and I couldn't possibly afford it if the company wasn't footing the bill.'

Inez studied her with gentle eyes and frowned. 'You have lost weight, I think.'

Laura held her smile in place, knowing the remark was prompted by genuine concern. Her shrug was over-casual. 'What do you expect? Most of my time off is spent scrambling about on the Upper Rock observing the apes and other wildlife for my articles. Anyway,' her tone changed, becoming brisker as she steered the conversation away from herself, 'I can't tell you how grateful I am for the loan of the typewriter. I could have hired one.'

Inez brushed the suggestion aside. 'For what—two hours? What was the point? This is our spare. I am only glad we could help. When will yours be mended?'

'Mr Cardona promised I'd have it back by the end of the week. Apparently he has had to order some special part for it.'

'Well, if you need this one again you have only to ask.' Inez tipped her head on one side, openly curious. 'Why don't you ask your secretary to do this typing for you?'

Laura pushed her hands into her pockets and turned her head to stare out at the teeming rain. The soft buzz of conversation eddied around them as guests came and went. She raised one shoulder, a shy, awkward movement. 'No, I can't, not yet. It's too ... personal somehow. Anyway,' she glanced sideways, a sudden grin lifting the corners of her mouth, 'there's never a moment's peace down there for Lisa *or* me. Mr Ansaldo from the Ministry of Economic Development and Trade was on the phone *three* times yesterday. It's common knowledge that he and my boss have different views on most matters, so guess who had to take the calls? *And* I'd already seen a delegation from the unions, plus one of the directors of the Chamber of Commerce.' Inez tutted sympathetically. 'Besides, understanding though Dennis is, even he would balk at my hobby invading Phoenix time and territory.' She patted the typewriter. 'Thanks again, Inez.' She turned to go.

'One moment, Laura. There is mail for you, I think.' In the office behind Inez a telephone rang. At the same moment the telex began to clatter. The other two receptionists were busy with a newly arrived party.

'Don't bother now,' Laura grimaced with understanding. 'I'll collect it later.'

'No,' Inez said at once. 'For our long-stay guests we are *more* caring, not less. You must wait just one second. It's not all sorted yet,' she called over her shoulder, 'but I saw your name on two, I think.'

The envelopes were placed in Laura's hand and, with a cheery wave, Inez disappeared once more into the office to answer the telephone's insistent summons. Laura heard her greet the caller with such charm and patience she might have been at the beginning rather than the end of a long busy day.

She started towards the little group of shops just inside the main entrance. If she didn't get Aunt Freda's birthday card off soon, it wouldn't reach her in time. Aunt Freda was special, her closest relative, discounting Gavin, and Laura couldn't bear the thought of her being disappointed.

She glanced at the top letter. The English stamps and her brother's flamboyant scrawl, so out of keeping with his work as a tax law consultant and his apparent shyness, lifted her spirits at once.

She hadn't heard from Gavin since the week after her arrival. It was understandable of course. In love for the first time in all his twenty-nine years, no doubt her quiet, brainy brother had far better things to do than write to *her*.

Smiling wistfully at the thought of Gavin in love, Laura hoped this letter would tell her a little more about the girl in question. The only *facts* she had been able to extract from Gavin's last scribble were that Cheryl was the same age as herself, twenty-five, and was 'something in the fashion world'. For a man whose whole career was based on accurate interpretation of words and figures, he had managed to tell her remarkably little. Sighing with wry amusement, Laura turned over the second letter.

At once her stomach knotted with tension as she stared at the neat, precise script. She swallowed a sudden dryness in her throat. What possible reason could Jeremy have for writing? And why send it here to the hotel? Why not the office address? For that was the only connection remaining between them, the fact that they both still worked for the same company. Everything had been said—everything necessary and far more than was pleasant.

Jostled from behind by a plump German woman who stopped scolding her squabbling children long enough to murmur an apology, Laura looked up as the main doors opened.

Tall and dark, he moved with the loose, easy stride of a man in prime physical condition. His two cases, though of excellent quality, looked much travelled, and rain had spotted the broad shoulders of his olive leather jacket.

Laura's mind clicked into top gear. Her letters forgotten, she watched him as he approached the desk. She knew she ought to know who he was. She recognised his face. But from where?

As he looked up to return Inez's greeting, Laura stared at the lean profile and sought desperately for a name. She saw straight black brows over eyes so dark they too looked black, an aquiline nose that had been broken at some time, and a wide mouth which, as he smiled, revealed strong, white, slightly uneven teeth. Deep lines scored the sides of his mouth and the corners of his eyes. His skin was bronzed with wind and sun yet, despite the outward appearance of controlled energy, Laura discerned utter weariness.

Glimpsing the quizzical look Inez flashed at her, she dismissed the thought at once. Her mind was playing tricks, reflecting *her* feelings on to the stranger. And yet . . .

He picked up his room key after signing the registration card and followed the porter carrying his cases towards the lift.

Laura returned quickly to the desk. 'Inez, who *is* he?' she whispered.

Inez could not mask her surprise. During the time Laura Jefford had been a guest at the hotel, their daily contact ripening into the warmth of friendship, she had never seen Laura give any man so much as a passing glance. She had often wondered at this, for Laura was an attractive girl, if a little slender for Spanish tastes, and clearly possessed a kind heart. But it was not her business and, aside from professional courtesy, consideration forbade that she ask questions, even though her intuition told her Laura had suffered great unhappiness quite recently.

'I know him,' Laura explained hurriedly, flushing rosily as she recognised the obvious interpretation of her interest. 'Professionally, I mean. I've seen him in connection with the company, but I can't remember where or when.' She looked around. The man had followed the porter into the lift. He turned, and, as the doors whispered shut, across the width of the reception area their eyes met.

The contact was fleeting, but its impact sufficient to unlock Laura's memory. Her heart pounded as it all flooded back. Belgium, two years ago.

She had been Dennis's secretary then, and a member of the company party visiting the new trans-shipment complex Phoenix was building in Antwerp docks. Jeremy had been with the party too. It was in Antwerp that he had first asked her to marry him. He had made a joke of it of course, but it had marked a new phase in his pursuit of her.

She should have realised then that things were not as they seemed. But Jeremy had been so charming, so persuasive. And she had been so naïve, believing all he said about admiring her grasp of the problems associated with port and harbour development, and especially her ability to get on with all the people concerned, from the shop stewards to the project manager.

She had not detected his jealousy, had not recognised the moment he had begun to undermine *her* confidence in an effort to build up his own. He had felt his own position threatened by Dennis's growing reliance on her. But not for him the obvious manoeuvring to get her out. Jeremy had been far more subtle. He had convinced her that he loved and wanted her. Like a leech he had drained her, mentally and emotionally. As her belief in herself diminished, eroded by inexplicable mistakes, messages that went astray, appointments not kept, so he had grown stronger, always sympathetic, protective, totally disarming. In the end she had almost been convinced that she should do what he wanted—marry him and give up the job that was clearly too much for her.

Almost, but not quite. It had been that fragment of doubt that had saved her, preventing the total submersion of her own personality beneath his. That, and the fleeting memory of a pair of cynical dark eyes of which she had been aware at several of the gatherings arranged during the trip. Eyes which, she had realised later with painful hindsight, had summed Jeremy up within moments of meeting him, and had observed her with the clinical interest of a scientist for a microscope slide.

Their introduction had been brief, and the few words exchanged so unmemorable as to be totally forgotten. Indeed she had scarcely been aware of his continued presence, so demanding had the schedule been. After they left Antwerp she had been unable to recall the rest of his face. But the expression in his eyes, an incisive blend of mockery and contempt, had remained with her, recurring at unexpected, and often inopportune, moments, holding her back from the final commitment to

Jeremy, much to her own bewilderment and his ill-concealed frustration.

She heard Inez's voice as if from a distance. 'His name is——'

'Brent Lewis,' Laura finished for her. 'Internationally renowned shipping journalist.'

'So,' Inez was clearly intrigued, 'he is famous.'

'His work is,' Laura said. 'His by-line is rarely out of *Lloyd's List* and the other maritime papers and magazines.'

Now she remembered who he was, the next question was automatic. Why was he *here*? A holiday? Possible but unlikely. It was mid-April, still the rainy season. But if he was here on business, it could be for only one reason, the proposed development of the harbour. That meant he was here to see *them*, Dennis and herself, as representatives of the Phoenix Group.

But if Dennis was expecting him, why hadn't he mentioned it? Maybe Dennis *didn't* know. Was Brent Lewis here on his own initiative, or had he been sent? If so, by whom?

'Laura? You are all right?' Inez's concern broke into her racing thoughts.

'Yes. Yes, I'm fine.' Her reply and her smile both lacked conviction, but before Inez could say more Laura gave her a brief wave and turned once more towards the shop. One thing at a time, and first on the list was Aunt Freda's card.

After all, if Brent Lewis *was* here on an assignment, it would be Dennis he would talk to. Dennis always dealt with the Press. He was marvellous at it, he said so himself. *She* would be left to cope with the Minister, the unions and that awful little man from the Chamber of Commerce who could not make up his mind whether to patronise her or make a pass!

Dennis frequently told her how much he relied upon her tact and diplomacy. And there was no doubt she had averted more than one crisis when conflicting ideas concerning project priorities had reached the eyeball-to-eyeball stage.

But where the Press was concerned, Dennis had no problems at all. Whether a standard release or a specific interview, Dennis invariably got favourable coverage. If Brent Lewis *was* here about the company's new project, Dennis would deal with him. There would be no reason for her and Brent Lewis to meet at all.

She recalled the moment their eyes had met before the lift swallowed him up. Still cynical, his gaze had held something else, a bitterness that had sent a chill like an icy finger down her spine. Yet it could not have been directed at her, for there had been no flicker of recognition.

Laura stared at the array of cards without seeing them. So much had changed in the past two years. Her position in the company for a start. As Dennis's personal assistant her responsibilities were far greater and more wide-ranging than they had been as his secretary. She even had a secretary of her own now!

Despite having got off to a very shaky start, a situation due, she realised now, to Jeremy's deliberate sabotage, she loved the challenge of her job and the uncertainty of never knowing what she would be called on to deal with next. It kept her mentally on her toes, and the adrenalin flowing. And if, once in a while, the pressure showed in a slight weight-loss and a tiredness that seemed to seep into her bones, it was a small price to pay for the return of her self-confidence. Or most of it.

There had been no one else in the fifteen months since she had finished with Jeremy. She had told herself it was simply lack of time. Her new job demanded far more of her and it was often more convenient to work on in the evenings when everyone else had gone and the telephones were blessedly silent. Being so busy she just didn't have time to feel lonely. Well, not often.

Besides, she owed Dennis so much. He had continued believing in her, even in the darkest days, when she had all but lost faith in herself. He had seemed to realise she was as bemused and shaken by what was happening to her as he was.

Then Jeremy had been sent to Rotterdam to replace the manager there who had had a heart attack. Laura had not understood his reluctance to go, for it was, in effect, a promotion. She had heard him arguing with Dennis. But he had been the only logical choice and Dennis had overruled every objection.

Strangely, things had taken a sudden turn for the better. Her work had begun to run smoothly, with none of the problems and mistakes she had come to dread. She had, at first, felt terribly guilty at the *relief* Jeremy's absence brought her; after all, had he not always been totally supportive and sympathetic? But the heady sensation of freedom, as though she had been freed from a suffocating prison, had set her thinking and led, after much anguished soul-searching, to her breaking off the engagement.

Even now she felt cold and sick when she recalled the dreadful scene her quietly voiced announcement had precipitated. Shying away from the memory, Laura concentrated on choosing the birthday card. Jeremy was no longer a part of her life. Nothing his letter contained was of interest to her. She was not the person he had known. She was her own woman again. She had trusted and had paid dearly, but the lesson had been well learned.

Though he would never know it, she had reason to be grateful to the cold, unapproachable Brent Lewis.

She looked down at Jeremy's unopened letter in her hand and, with a swift, decisive movement, tore it across twice. Dropping the pieces into the litter-bin by the door, she took a deep, calming breath and, a couple of minutes later, found the perfect card for Aunt Freda.

The next morning, following her normal practice, Laura walked into Dennis's office just after ten. She was carrying her desk diary, several letters and two bulging files.

Glimpsing her reflection in the glass covering the huge aerial photograph of the harbour hanging on the wall, she smothered a wry smile. In total contrast to the previous day, she now looked every inch the sophisticated career-girl in her smart grey and red shirt-dress and matching red high heels. Make-up was a necessary part of her public image and, though light, it added depth to her blue eyes, a hint of colour to her high cheekbones, and lustre to the gentle contours of her mouth. She had confined her wayward, golden-brown hair to a coil high on her head, but as always, tendrils had escaped to curl softly on her neck and temples.

Without waiting to exchange their usual greetings and banter about which of them had the busiest schedule that day, Dennis waved a piece of paper which looked as though it had been crumpled into a ball before an unsuccessful attempt had been made to smooth it out again. 'Have I got news for you.' His normally cheerful face was set and grim as he gestured for her to sit down.

'Didn't you know he was coming, then?' Laura settled herself in the comfortable armchair on the opposite side of the desk and tried to ignore a frisson of apprehension. She was still a little tired. Though she had destroyed Jeremy's letter unread, its very arrival had unsettled her, stirring up the past and memories she had tried so hard to forget.

Dennis frowned. 'Who?'

'Brent Lewis, of course.'

'Lewis?' Dennis was clearly taken aback. 'What the hell's he doing here?'

Laura's heart sank. 'I was hoping you knew. He booked into my hotel late yesterday afternoon.'

'Damn!' Dennis muttered explosively. 'He can't have got wind of it already. God, that man is like a tracker dog.'

'What?' Perplexity furrowed Laura's forehead. 'What's happened, Dennis? What are you talking about?'

'Sorry, Laura, but you're going to have to deal with him.'

'*Me?*' Laura sat bolt upright in her chair. 'But *you* have always handled the Press.'

'Unfortunately, that won't be possible this time.' Dropping the letter on to his desk, Dennis leaned on his elbows, rubbing his forehead with his fingertips.

'Why?' Laura began, not understanding. 'You——'

'Because I won't *be* here.'

'*What?*' Her voice rose an octave.

'Read it,' Dennis ordered wearily, pushing the letter towards her. 'On second thoughts, don't waste your time. What it boils down to is problems with funding for the project. Our merchant bank backers are digging their heels in and I have to return to London and convince them that we need the amount and frequency of the stage payments increased. The preliminary surveys have been completed and test drilling on the site for the new wharf is under way. We *can't* pull out now, but we must have more money.'

Laura forgot her own problems as the gravity of the situation facing the company sunk in. 'You think Brent Lewis *knows* about this?'

Dennis shrugged and reached to one side of his crowded desk for his cigarettes and lighter. Inhaling deeply, he blew a plume of smoke towards the ceiling. 'If he does, and he decides to print not only what he *knows*, but what he *speculates* the outcome might be, it could do the company, and the group, a lot of damage. You know as well as I do that these projects are as much about prestige as about hard cash. That applies to both the port *and* the company doing the job. The eyes of the shipping world are on Gibraltar at the moment. What with the border re-opening, the privatisation of the naval dockyard and the huge development programme, the Rock is attracting far more than its fair share of Press attention. Confidence is what counts in business. If confidence in *this* company is compromised, it could rebound on our associates within the group and——' He broke off and drew heavily on his cigarette.

Laura saw only too clearly. She saw something else too. Dennis had been working even longer hours than she. This project was his baby. He had conceived it, nurtured it and brought it to fruition. He was closer to it than anyone else. Too close perhaps.

'Look, it's possible he *doesn't* know.' Unable to sit still any longer, she began pacing the floor, passing the windows that looked down on to the old quarter known as Irish Town, and out towards the harbour. The water was steel-grey as heavy low cloud, driven by the westerly wind, heralded more rain. 'There's no reason why he should.' Absently, she rubbed her upper arms while her brain raced. 'Everything is all right at the Ministry. The drilling is on schedule and there are no labour problems. Have you any idea where he's come from?'

Dennis inhaled again and tapped his cigarette on the edge of an ashtray already containing four half-smoked stubs. 'He had an article in *Lloyd's List* a couple of weeks ago.' He screwed up his eyes in an effort to remember. 'I think—no, I'm sure, it was on one of the Canadian ports.'

Laura stopped pacing. 'Well, if he's come direct from Canada, he certainly won't have had time to listen to any whispers on the grapevine, even assuming there are any.'

Dennis ground out his cigarette, then slumped back in his chair, his stocky, shirt-sleeved figure revealing the softening of late middle age, his hands hanging loosely over the leather arms.

'Now I know why I keep you around, Laura,' he grinned at her. 'It's not just that quick brain of yours, it's your down-to-earth common sense.'

Laura snapped her fingers in mock disappointment, grinning back. 'And I thought it was my body you were after.'

Laughing aloud, Dennis stood up and, pulling his jacket from the back of the chair, slipped it on. 'If I were twenty years younger ...' He shook his head.

It was an empty threat and they both knew it. Dennis's abiding love for his wife and three daughters fulfilled him completely and had him flying home for visits at every opportunity.

To Laura he was a special blend of boss, friend, teacher and the father she could not remember. Her fond admiration for him and the respect and liking she had developed for his wife precluded anything other than a strictly professional relationship. Yet within those bounds, she and Dennis were about as close as it was possible to be. They trusted one another totally, and

Laura knew he was guiding and grooming her for further promotion within the group.

Dennis pulled his large diary towards him. 'I'm off to the bank in half an hour. I've cancelled all my appointments for this afternoon, and you'll have to see Otilio about checking the core samples.'

Laura looked up from her own diary. 'How soon do you plan to go?'

'My plane leaves for Gatwick at ten tomorrow morning. I'm sorry Laura,' he repeated, as she tried to disguise her visible shock. 'But the sooner I can get this business sorted out, the sooner I'll be back. Now,' he lifted his briefcase on to the desk and began to sort files and letters from the mass of paperwork littering its surface, slotting them into the case, 'about Lewis.'

Laura felt her heart kick and her fingers tightened on her pen as she finished making a note.

'You must stick to him like glue. I mean it, Laura. Cancel everything that's not absolutely vital. Take him around, make sure he meets everyone he asks about, but *you* make the introductions. Show him not only the harbour and the project, but the rest of the Rock as well. Let him see how our plans will benefit the whole community. Increased trade means more jobs, greater affluence, you know the sort of thing. He's got a lot of weight, Laura. His reports are read in the City as well as the shipping world. He could influence investment, not only now but for the future as well. So make yourself indispensable. The company is in your hands. I'm relying on you.'

Laura clutched her diary like a life-belt as the enormity of what Dennis was asking dawned on her. She recalled dark, cynical eyes. Eyes that were cold and bitter. She swallowed. Then she noticed the sheen of perspiration on Dennis's forehead and upper lip, and the sudden greyness of his normally ruddy complexion, and momentarily forgot her own fears.

'Dennis? Are you all right?'

'Touch of indigestion, that's all.' He rubbed his rib cage, trying to smile. 'All this rushing about is enough to put anyone off their food.' He snapped his briefcase shut and looked at his watch. Sinking down into his chair he took the handkerchief from his breast pocket and mopped his brow.

'Shall I get you——' Laura was interrupted by the buzzing of the intercom. Glancing at Dennis, who nodded, she pressed the switch. 'Yes, Josefa?'

'There is a Mr Brent Lewis to see Mr Sanderson. He doesn't have an appointment but——'

'One moment please, Josefa.' Laura flicked the switch to Hold.

'He's a cunning devil,' Dennis muttered, and to Laura's astonishment she detected a hint of admiration.

'Surely you don't have to see him now? Let him make an appointment like everyone else.'

'But he isn't *everyone else*,' Dennis pointed out, tucking the handkerchief away and sitting up straighter. The colour was slowly returning to his cheeks. 'He knows that and so do we. It's going to appear mighty suspicious if I refuse to see him now and take the first plane out in the morning. Don't look like that,' he warned. 'Brent Lewis isn't some power-hungry little hack. He's the ultimate professional. I would do exactly the same in his place. He wanted to catch us on the hop. He *expects* to be turned away, which is why we're not going to do it.' Dennis flicked the intercom switch. 'Please ask Mr Lewis to come in, Josefa.' He stood up, squaring his shoulders. 'It's up to you now, Laura.'

Closing her diary, Laura laid it on top of the files she had brought in. Her heart began to pound as adrenalin flooded her system. She ran unsteady hands over her hips, smoothing her dress, mentally bracing herself for the enormous responsibility Dennis had just laid on her. She drew in a deep breath. 'I won't let you down,' she promised softly.

The door opened.

CHAPTER TWO

As Josefa closed the door softly behind him, Brent Lewis walked forward to shake Dennis's proffered hand. There was an air about him, Laura couldn't define it, yet the office seemed suddenly smaller. Casually dressed in tobacco-coloured cords, cream open-necked shirt and a pine-green sweater flecked with black and orange, he seemed totally at ease, even sympathetic. 'Good of you to see me, especially under the circumstances.'

Her senses finely tuned by nervous tension, Laura realised at once that Dennis had not exaggerated: she would need to keep her wits about her. Brent Lewis was an attractive man. He was also cunning. His deep voice and naturally slow manner of speaking soothed, inviting confidences. But Dennis had been around too long to fall into the trap.

'What circumstances?' he enquired with an innocent smile. 'If you mean your lack of an appointment, don't give it another thought, we're always delighted to assist the Press. After all, we need you as much as you need us. As a matter of fact, you couldn't have timed it better.' He glanced at his watch. 'I have a few minutes before my next appointment. However, before we get down to what brings you to the Rock,' he turned to draw Laura forward, 'you must meet my personal assistant.'

Laura steeled herself to avoid flinching under his powerful scrutiny, schooling her features into a polite smile. The eyes she had thought black were, in fact, very dark brown. They seemed to pierce her very soul, yet revealed nothing of the man behind them.

'Don't I know you?' His brows formed a thick bar as he frowned.

Feeling as though she was stepping off the topmost diving-board not knowing how far down it was to the water, Laura extended her hand. 'I believe we have met, Mr Lewis. In Antwerp, two years ago.'

He did not release her hand at once and Laura was aware of a tingling warmth, a current arcing between them, and a new mouth-drying awareness of him as a man.

'I—I doubt you'd remember. M-most of my work was done behind the scenes.' She strove to steady her voice, she *had* to conquer her nerves, for Dennis's sake. But coping with Brent Lewis was going to demand far more of her than she had ever imagined. She had remembered his eyes, but not the sheer force of his personality, though she instinctively knew he was making no effort to impress. He had no need to. 'I was Mr Sanderson's secretary then.'

'How could I forget?' One corner of Brent's mouth lifted in a disconcerting smile. 'And now you're his personal assistant. That's quite a leap in two years.'

His tone had not changed, but Laura felt her hackles rise. Perhaps she was being over-sensitive. After all, she was no stranger to snide remarks and the insinuation that her rapid promotion owed less to her brain than her body. Determinedly, she shrugged aside her anger. Allowing Brent Lewis to ruffle her would give him an advantage, and on no account could she afford that. She met his gaze with as much serenity as she could muster. 'Yes, isn't it.'

'Laura's my right arm,' Dennis announced, smiling at her. 'She knows as much about this project as I do, so anything you want to know, just ask her.'

'Why not you?' Brent queried with deceptive mildness. Laura held her breath. How would Dennis handle it? How much or how little would he reveal?

'I'm off to London in the morning,' he beamed. 'A few routine meetings then a day or two relaxing with my family.'

'So, no problems with the project then?'

'Do you think I'd be leaving if there were?' Dennis twinkled, ridiculing the very idea. 'No,' he rubbed his hands, an open display of satisfaction, 'we're right on target. I'm sure Laura, Miss Jefford, would be delighted to take you down to the site so you can see for yourself. I'm assuming you are here to cover the development programme?'

Brent nodded. 'Both *Lloyd's List* and Marine Publications want a series of in-depth articles.'

Dennis and Laura exchanged the briefest of glances. Laura swallowed hard. This was it. She took the plunge. 'Then on behalf of Phoenix Development, allow me to welcome you to Gibraltar. Perhaps I could offer you lunch and a guided tour of our own project.'

'How kind.' Brent's politeness matched her own but his dark eyes held an irony that brought warmth to her cheeks. 'However, I'm afraid I'll have to defer that pleasure until tomorrow. I have one or two other things lined up today. What time would suit you, Miss—I'm terribly sorry, I didn't catch your name.'

So that's the way it's going to be, Laura thought. Well, you're used to dealing with men like him, arrogant, patronising, chauvinistic—she caught herself. He wasn't just another man. It wouldn't do to forget that this one, despite his undoubted attractiveness and a voice as soothing as liquid honey, had the instincts of a piranha.

'Jefford, Mr Lewis, Laura Jefford.' She understood his reputation more clearly now. No one would ever *assume* with Brent Lewis, nor take anything about him for granted. If only there had been more warning and she had had a little longer to prepare herself.

Checking her diary, she was relieved to find there was nothing arranged for the following day that could not be postponed. 'Would ten o'clock suit you, Mr Lewis?'

'So early?' One dark brow arched. 'Surely you have more important matters to attend to?'

Laura resisted the urge to turn pleading eyes to Dennis. She forced herself to smile. 'Mr Lewis, when a journalist as widely known and respected as yourself turns up to investigate expansion plans such as those under way here in Gibraltar, no company with any sense would have *more important matters* to attend to. Governments and private investors in places as far apart as Hong Kong and the oil states of the Middle East read your reports.'

'And you intend to ensure my view of Phoenix Development is a favourable one?'

She recognised, as he clearly intended she should, the several shades of meaning embodied in his question. Antagonism flared between them, sharp, almost crackling, in the already tense atmosphere.

She longed to tell him she didn't give a damn about his views, that if she never laid eyes on him again it would be far too soon. Then common sense reasserted itself and, with it, puzzlement. She had very good reasons for being on edge, defensive even. But why was *he* so...so...angry?

'I can only show you what we are achieving, Mr Lewis,' Laura said with icy politeness. 'I would not dream of trying to influence your opinions.' She sent up a mental prayer for forgiveness.

His eyes gleamed momentarily. 'Indeed.' He injected just enough sarcasm to make it sound like a question.

Laura continued as if he had not spoken. 'We must rely upon your integrity to present a fair and accurate picture.'

The silence stretched. Laura felt a stab of fear. Had she gone too far?

'No one has ever questioned my integrity.' His very quietness had cold fingers clawing at Laura's stomach.

Screwing up her courage she met his gaze. 'Then no one has ever had cause. Ten o'clock, Mr Lewis?'

'I'll be here.'

It sounded to Laura like a threat, but she dismissed the notion as a product of the strain she was under.

'I feel I'm throwing you to the sharks, well, one particular shark,' Dennis said, his face creased with worry, after the door had closed on Brent's tall figure.

Aware of how much Dennis already had on his plate, Laura brushed aside his concern with a confidence she did not feel. 'Come on, you've trained me to deal with far worse situations that this. I'm not underestimating him, Dennis,' a sudden shiver brought goosepimples up on her arms, 'far from it. But you heard the man. He's here to do a whole series of articles. That will involve a lot of meetings and an enormous amount of work. He simply won't have time to waste on speculation about our company.'

'I just wish I didn't have to go *now*,' Dennis groaned, adding hurriedly, 'It's not that I don't——'

'I know,' Laura interrupted gently and picked up her paperwork. 'But we have no choice. You *do* have to go. Look, is there anything you can tell me about him, anything that might be useful?'

Dennis leaned back in his chair, wincing slightly and absently rubbing his breastbone. 'I've had dealings with the man for over ten years and I can't say I even begin to know what makes him tick. He's a damn good journalist, one of the best in his field, but as a person...' He shrugged. 'He gives nothing away, and he's not the sort of man to invite questions. He's not married, that I do know.'

'That doesn't surprise me,' Laura snorted. For all his looks and that hypnotic voice, there was a coldness, an unapproachability about Brent Lewis.

'Hang on,' Dennis warned, 'he had quite a reputation as a ladies' man at one time. Never out of the gossip columns, according to my wife. God knows if half of it's true, you know what the papers are. But if it is, my guess would be that affairs were conducted on *his* terms with a bunch of flowers and a kiss goodbye the instant *she* started hearing wedding-bells.'

'Dennis!' Laura exclaimed. 'Do I detect a note of envy?'

'What do you think?' he retorted, grinning.

'Anyway,' Laura was intrigued despite herself, 'what do you mean, *at one time*? He's only, what, thirty-four? Thirty-five? That's not exactly decrepit.'

'Apparently he got engaged about a year ago, to a fashion designer. My wife keeps me up to date on all such important matters. The girl was very talented by all accounts, had a client list that read like *Who's Who*, and she was only twenty-four.'

'You keep saying *was*. What happened? Oh, lord, she didn't die, did she?'

Dennis shook his head. 'She walked out on him. It must have been six months or so ago. That hit the gossip columns too as, apparently, there was someone else involved. But they both kept pretty tight-lipped about it.

Anyway, since then, judging by his output, he's taken every foreign assignment offered.'

Laura had a vivid image of Brent entering the hotel foyer, and of the utter weariness she sensed in him. She felt a moment's compassion but swiftly banished it. If he had been fooling around while he was engaged, no wonder his fiancée had walked out.

Always on the move, living out of a suitcase, totally independent, arrogant, demanding, tyrannical, he would be hell to live with. And yet, for a brief moment, unaware he was being observed, he had looked oddly vulnerable. With a tiny pang she recalled the warmth of his smile for Inez. There had been no such pleasure in his greeting of Dennis and herself. In fact, looking back, as they had shaken hands he had seemed for an instant taken aback.

This was ridiculous, she admonished herself. Brent Lewis's private life was none of her concern. Why should she care whether he smiled or not? The last thing she wanted was him lulling her into a false sense of security. He could be as rude and taciturn as he chose; in some ways it would make her job far easier.

'I'd better get moving,' Dennis broke into her thoughts. 'I'm due at the bank and there are several other things I must see to before I go. I'll catch you later this afternoon.'

Laura nodded and went to the door. 'Good luck,' she smiled at him.

He grimaced. 'I've a feeling we're both going to need it.'

That evening, unable to concentrate on the papers crowding her desk and, for the first time, unwilling to remain in the office alone, Laura hurried back to the hotel. After a light meal in the coffee-shop she returned to her room, took a quick shower and slipped into a lounging robe of midnight-blue velvet, leaving her hair loose over her shoulders.

It was too early for bed. In any case she was too keyed up to sleep. She switched on the television, but after only a minute, switched it off again. Crossing to the writing-table she picked up the photographs of black kites, marsh harriers and Egyptian vultures she had taken from the upper cable-car station two weeks previously. It had been an amazing sight as the birds' migration flight carried them in their thousands almost at rooftop height over the rock. Why didn't she begin drafting the next article?

But after half an hour and several false starts, Laura tossed her pad and pencil on to the table. Pushing back her chair, she went to the window. Now she was free to relax, she couldn't.

The heavy clouds had parted long enough for the setting sun to flame the sky with orange and gold. Now, darkness was falling.

Since she had first arrived in Gibraltar, this room, so tastefully furnished in subtle shades of pink and grey, had been her haven, her escape from the inevitable pressures of her job. She had, by adding books, flowers, framed photographs and an ornament or two, made it more personal and homely. But tonight she felt trapped. Yet where could she go? Who could she talk to?

She was here at the Holiday Inn while Dennis was at the Rock Hotel. She had appreciated his thoughtfulness. Had they shared a hotel, meeting at breakfast and dinner, conversation would inevitably have turned to business. 'You need time to yourself, time to meet new people, make new friends,' he had said.

But the emotional bruises were still too fresh and apart from Inez, Laura had avoided involvement, keeping her contact with the people she saw regularly friendly but distant.

Right now she would willingly have talked contracts and schedules for the sake of Dennis's company.

She stared out over the rising tiers of brightly lit houses to the shadowy mass of the Rock itself.

The most southerly point in Europe, it stood sentinel at the junction of Atlantic and Mediterranean.

Laura tried to visualise the conquering Moor who, thirteen hundred years ago, had changed the face of this towering piece of limestone.

Tall, dark-skinned, in turban, breastplate and flowing robes, Tarik ibn Ziad, commanding an army of Arabs and Berbers, had crossed the narrow strait from North Africa to invade the Rock. After building fortifications they had surged on to capture, within a few months, almost the whole of Spain. He had given the Rock a name, his name, Jebel Tarik—Tarik's Mountain.

Instead of the bearded Moor, the stern features of Brent Lewis filled her mind, his piercing brown eyes agleam with mockery, and an ironic twist to his mouth.

Jumping as though she had been stung, Laura quickly drew the curtains, shutting out the night and the view. Then she lifted the heavy fall of hair from her neck. She was suddenly very warm and it clung damply. He was no threat, no aggressive invader. He was here simply to do his job.

But, an inner voice reminded her, it was a job in which *she* was deeply involved, a job with which she had to both help *and hinder* him.

She pressed her palms to her throbbing temples and tried desperately to force him from her mind. Tomorrow morning would come all too soon.

She sank down on to the edge of the large bed, her eye caught by Gavin's letter lying on the bedside table. She read it once more, and the corners of her mouth lifted. Her brother's happiness burst from every line.

He was bringing Cheryl over to meet her. They intended to make the visit part of their honeymoon trip. He realised the mention of marriage would come as something of a shock but Cheryl was *the* one, and neither of them wanted to wait any longer. They had met at a party neither had been keen to attend, but had recognised something in each other and that had been that.

So simple, Laura thought wistfully. She was delighted for him, for both of them. Then something clicked. Her hand fell into her lap and, still holding the letter, she gazed blindly at the wall opposite. *No.* The idea was ridiculous, too silly even to contemplate. Coincidence just didn't stretch that far.

She raised the letter again and this time the words took on a new and dreadful significance.

'Cheryl's so much in demand,' she read, 'she's even been invited to submit designs for one of a certain Royal Highness's visits abroad. But keep that to yourself, one's not supposed to gossip about these things. She desperately needs a holiday, poor love. Life has been very fraught for her this last year. No, I don't mean meeting me, dear sister! She says the six months we've been together have been the happiest in her life. It was what happened before. She won't talk about it, but if I ever get my hands on the swine who made her so unhappy——' Laura looked up, crushing the letter. She began to pace the room.

It *couldn't* be. It just wasn't possible. Her brother's wife-to-be and Brent Lewis's ex-fiancée one and the same?

But even as she scorned the idea, Dennis's description echoed clearly in her head '...*fashion designer...very talented...client list like* Who's Who...*only twenty-four.*' And they had broken up *six months ago*.

Laura closed her eyes. Did Brent know about his ex-fiancée's new love? He'd been away from England on foreign assignments for some time. But he had hundreds of contacts in the newspaper world, and Cheryl, if it *was* her, was a rising star, therefore newsworthy. Sooner or later some 'friend' would tell him, if they hadn't already.

Perhaps he did know, and perhaps he knew *who* the man was. Could that be why he had been so cold?

Laura clenched her fists. Weren't things difficult enough already? How was she supposed to deal with *this*?

Her thoughts flew to her brother. Older than her by four years, he had been the one shining beacon during the dark times of her life.

When their father had been killed trying to rescue a child after a train derailment and their mother was immersed in her own grief, it was Gavin who had comforted her.

When their mother's despair had slid into clinical depression and withdrawal from the world, it was Gavin Laura had clung to. Gavin had met her off the train from boarding-school at holiday times and allowed her to tag along to discos and barbecues, letting her find her own way, but ready to warn and protect when necessary.

After her mother's death, caused, so the doctor said, by bronchial pneumonia, but in Laura's view by sheer lack of will to live, Gavin had dealt with all the arrangements and seen her safely settled with a welcoming Aunt Freda before returning to university. He had always been her friend and confidant, the only person she had told about the fiasco with Jeremy. But right now she wished with all her heart he *wasn't* coming to see her.

Her ragged sigh was loud in the silence as she refolded the letter. Then she straightened up. She was allowing her imagination to run riot. Gavin had not given a date for their arrival, but given his own business commitments, and the obvious pressure of work on Cheryl, surely it was unlikely to be for at least a month?

Brent Lewis would have gone long before then.

In the meantime, her job was to assist him while protecting the company. To do that she would need every ounce of concentration. She could not afford to waste time and energy worrying about situations that were none of her concern, and problems that were unlikely to arise. She would say nothing, pretend she knew nothing. After all, she *could* be wrong.

Sitting down at the table, she picked up her pencil and the photographs. It was a long time before she began to write.

In his room along the corridor, Brent Lewis leaned against the balcony, nursing a drink. Light spilled over him from the open sliding window and the sounds of the town drifted up from below as his gaze rose from the buildings to the dark mass of rock above.

What the hell was he doing here? In four weeks he was due to go to Hong Kong. Instead of taking this job, which meant at least a week of intensive research and interviews, then another two transferring it all into copy, he should be stretched out on a beach somewhere *quiet*, doing absolutely nothing but rediscovering the art of relaxing. He needed this kind of pressure about as much as he needed a hole in the head. So why had he accepted the job?

He didn't have anything to prove. He certainly didn't need the money. *Habit*. The answer sprang unbidden, surprising, into his mind. It was easier to keep moving than to stop and think.

He raised the glass, his eyes narrowing as the spirit burned its way down.

What was there to think about? He had a job he enjoyed and was good at, an extremely healthy bank
balance, and opportunities for unlimited travel.

So why did he no longer get the same kick out of it?

Everyone had their off-days.

For six months?

It had nothing to do with that, with her.

Oh no? The argument flew back and forth in his head.

No. The break-up was inevitable.

So, you're finally admitting you were wrong?

I never denied it.

He tried to recall the face of the girl he had once
thought he loved but, like mist, it dissolved and he saw
instead with startling clarity, large blue-green eyes fringed
with thick lashes, tawny hair he had an overwhelming
urge to release from its restricting coil and run his hands
through, and a heart-shaped face with a determined little
chin below a generous and gently curving mouth that
looked ripe to be kissed.

He took another pull at his drink. She had changed
in those two years. There was a new strength about her,
a quiet confidence which even her nervousness could not
entirely hide.

During an interview in Rotterdam a couple of months
ago, Jeremy Grainger had let slip that she was unstable,
and trying to do a job that was beyond her.

That wasn't his impression, but he'd get a clearer
picture of the truth during the next couple of weeks.
Why *was* she nervous? What did she have to hide? He'd
find out, one way or another.

His jaw tightened. The attraction had been instant,
startling. And, judging by the sudden widening of those
beautiful eyes when they had shaken hands, not entirely
one-sided. His stay in Gibraltar might be more entertaining than he had anticipated.

He stared for a moment into the glass, then tossed back the remainder of his drink as though it were taken for its numbing effect rather than pleasure. The half-smile playing at the corner of his mouth was at odds with the bleakness in his eyes.

At five minutes to ten the following morning, Laura closed the last file and handed it to her secretary. 'That's all for now, Lisa. Do you have enough to keep you busy for the rest of the day, just in case I don't get back this afternoon?'

Lisa pulled a comic face. 'There's enough here for the rest of the week, so don't rush.' Scooping up the heap of files, she staggered towards the door. Laura leaped up and opened it for her.

Alone once more, Laura stretched her arms above her head and arched her back, trying to ease the tension that lay across her shoulders like an iron bar. Too tense to sleep well, she had got up soon after six. The warm shower had relaxed her. Then she had flicked the dial, gasping as the icy spray needled her body, clearing her head and making her skin tingle.

For several minutes she had agonised over what to wear. It had nothing to do with vanity. She was representing the company and she could not afford to allow Brent Lewis the opportunity of using whatever she was wearing as an excuse to ditch her while he went off to start asking questions elsewhere.

The air was soft and sweet, and a gentle breeze rippled like silk over her skin as she looked out of the open window. Yesterday's rain clouds had gone and the sky was a clear pale blue.

Despite her apprehension, the beauty of the spring morning lifted her spirits as she stepped into white linen slacks, an orange silk tunic bloused over a broad white belt fastened loosely on her hips, and white sandals. Gold stud earrings and a fine gold chain were her only jewellery. After sweeping her hair up into the usual coil, she applied mascara and lip-gloss then stood back, appraising her reflection with critical eyes.

Maybe she should have dressed more formally. She banished the momentary doubt. Skirts and high heels were hardly practical for visiting the dock area and the wharf.

After a quick breakfast of coffee and rolls she had arrived at the office just before eight and worked solidly until a few moments ago.

Laura glanced at her watch. The minute hand was almost on twelve. Leaning over she picked up her bag, intending to make a last-minute check of her appearance, just to reassure herself. But there was a tap on the door and Lisa poked her head around.

'Mr Lewis is here.'

Swiftly, Laura put the little mirror away, and replaced her bag beside her chair, moistening lips that were suddenly dry. Her heart fluttered like a trapped bird as she stood up, keeping the desk between herself and the door. 'Ask——' She cleared her throat. 'Ask him to come in.'

And there he was. Lisa vanished. For a moment neither of them spoke. Laura felt the room shrink.

He was wearing olive-green trousers that moulded his lean hips and long legs, and a matching short-sleeved shirt open at the neck to reveal dark hair curling crisply at the base of his throat. His face, neck and arms were a uniform bronze and it occurred to Laura that he was probably the same colour all over. Warmth flooded her face and she looked quickly away as she rounded the desk to greet him.

'Good morning, Mr Lewis. You are prompt.'

He looked quizzical. 'Weren't you ready for me? You did say ten.'

Laura could have kicked herself. 'Ready and waiting,' she said lightly.

He smiled as he took her hand. 'As we are going to be working so closely for the next couple of weeks, would it not save time if we used first names?'

Laura retrieved her hand from the warmth of his firm clasp as warning bells clamoured.

'My impression yesterday was that you preferred formality,' her voice was cool.

'Changed my mind,' he shrugged with a disarming grin.

Why? Laura wondered, but did not ask. 'As you wish.' She turned to her desk and picked up her small appointment book, then reached for her bag, willing the tremor from her hands. 'I suggest we go to the wharf first.'

'First?' His dark eyes gleamed.

Laura swallowed hard. 'You're going to need to talk to a lot of people. Phoenix has those contacts. I can save you a lot of time, and that's what you're after, isn't it?'

His slow smile crawled along her nerves. 'Among other things.'

As they reached the street, Laura raised her hand to hail a taxi, but Brent waved it past. 'It's a glorious day, let's walk. You can tell me about the place.'

'I thought you were in a hurry,' Laura quipped drily. 'There's a lot to tell.'

'Necessary background,' he countered, looking around at the tall, stone-faced buildings with their ornate balconies of black wrought iron, the tubs and pots of jewel-bright geraniums, and walls festooned with purple bougainvillaea. Worn steps and narrow alleys connected with the lower roads and provided tantalising glimpses of the harbour and the sea beyond, sapphire-blue and sparkling in the sunshine. 'How long have you been here?'

'Two months.' Seeing irony in the way he nodded, she added, 'I did quite a bit of reading, history and so on, before I came, and I've done a lot more since. And, naturally, I've explored, visiting the caves, the museum and the Tower of Homage.'

'Naturally,' he agreed.

Laura felt her hackles rising at his tone. 'Gibraltar's history is fascinating,' she continued, gritting her teeth. 'Do you know of any other piece of rock with an area of two and three-quarter square miles which has been fought over by——' she ticked off on her fingers '——the Phoenicians, Romans, Visigoths, Moors, Spanish and British? The town is eighteenth-century Regency built on fifteenth-century Spanish which in turn was built over a twelfth-century Moorish town.' She recalled her vision of Brent Lewis's features superimposed on those of Tarik ibn Ziad, the Moorish invader, and went on hurriedly, 'However, *my* main interest is the wildlife.'

Brent eyed her and the corners of his mouth twisted. 'You don't look the type.'

Used though she was to walking, Laura was almost having to run to match Brent's long stride. He seemed oblivious to her discomfort and she had no intention of admitting she found it hard to keep up. 'Is there a type?'

'For nightclubs? Discos? Gambling? I'd have said so.' His gaze was thoughtful, appraising, and held a spark of laughter. 'Not your scene at all.'

Confused, Laura didn't know how to react. Then, anger welled up. How dared he made assumptions? He knew nothing about her. 'As a matter of fact, I adore discos and nightclubs,' she retorted, ignoring the fact that she hadn't been to either since her arrival, or for months before that. 'However, I said wildlife, not nightlife.'

'What, plants, animals, that sort of thing?' Needled by his amused smile, Laura didn't notice the sharpening interest in his eyes. 'Why?'

'Why not?'

'A girl like you? You must have a reason.'

What did he mean? *A girl like her?* 'Two, actually,' she responded crisply. 'I write articles about the Rock's ecology, and I find birds and animals better company than some of the people I've been forced to deal with the past few years.'

His dark brows lifted fractionally, but he made no comment. Laura could almost hear his brain working, and the realisation of just how much she had let slip washed over her like icy water. She quickly turned her head, searching in her bag for her sunglasses.

It had taken them only minutes to walk from the office to the harbour yet already Brent Lewis had learned things she hadn't even told Dennis.

She steeled herself. Would he make the obvious retort, that if she couldn't stand the heat she should get out of the kitchen? Or would he simply continue his fiendishly clever probing, extracting information by goading her, keeping her off balance? But she was ready now, poised to deflect all personal questions.

He didn't give her a chance. 'Laura,' he asked conversationally as they passed the custom house and started towards the viaduct which would take them on to the north mole, 'just how comprehensive is this development programme?'

The sudden change of subject took her by surprise even as she was trying to ignore the way he had made her name sound almost like a caress. As she struggled to adjust, she realised that was undoubtedly his intention. *Right,* she thought.

'Very,' was her succinct reply. 'The Government has suddenly realised the enormous potential the Rock has in commercial terms. Off-shore banking, trans-shipment, crew-change facilities, and especially the development of the tourist trade now the border with Spain is open again. Last year there were two and a half million visitors, four times as many as in 1984.'

Brent nodded, glanced to his right and laid one hand gently on her arm as he indicated the smaller, much older-looking wharf. 'Was that the original port area?'

Laura nodded. His fingers burned through the fine silk of her shirt and she bent down to remove a non-existent stone from her sandals, not meeting his eye as she straightened up. 'It's still the focal point of the port's commercial activity. You can see the bonded warehouses and storage sheds. The car and passenger ferry to Tangier and the hydrofoil also berth there.'

Seagulls wheeled overhead, their cries blending with the sound of machinery, the throb and whine of engines and the hiss of steam. All around them ships were being unloaded, cargoes shifted, and stores delivered.

'So,' he gave her a slow, lazy smile which filled her with apprehension, 'what is Phoenix's part in all this?'

'We're building a roll-on roll-off berth which will take the pressure off the container-handling facilities. The project involves reclamation of land to the west of the north mole. You can see the drilling rig from here. The core samples so far indicate the sea bed is sound and perfectly capable of supporting the planned construction.' Laura stopped and surreptitiously took a deep breath. She had been talking faster and faster. But surely the worst was over now. 'All the plans are back at the office together with the geologist's report. You might like to look at them later.'

'Indeed I would.' He smiled again. 'One thing always fascinates me about projects like this,' he gazed around, taking in the whole dock area. 'Who pays for it? Where does the money come from?'

Laura's heart missed a beat.

CHAPTER THREE

LAURA glanced at him, grateful for the protection of her dark glasses. They started walking again. His hands in his pockets, Brent appeared totally relaxed. He might have been out simply for a leisurely stroll in the spring sunshine.

'The usual sources,' she answered lightly. 'Development grants, backed by merchant banks and private investment. Actually, that's Dennis's province. I deal more with the day-to-day practicalities.' He said nothing and she waited, her tension growing. Would he make the connection between Dennis's responsibility for the project's finance and his absence?

'Rather an unusual job for a woman, isn't it?'

Her fingers tightened on the strap of her bag. She kept her smile in place but could not entirely banish the frost from her tone. 'I don't think so.'

'Not defensive, surely?'

'Why should I be?'

'Why indeed? You know,' he observed. 'I don't see you as a flag-waver for the feminist cause.' His expression was a mixture of curiosity and amusement, yet she sensed he was not laughing *at* her. 'Of course, I could be wrong.'

'Coming from you that's quite an admission,' she retorted. Suddenly, much to her own amazement, Laura felt the tension drain away. He seemed to have accepted her claim that company finance was outside her sphere of responsibility and was apparently prepared to drop the subject. Her relief was heartfelt. Trying to maintain

42

such a high level of suspicion was exhausting, and she simply did not have the reserves. She saw one dark brow lift in response to her remark, and quashed a tiny spark of dangerous excitement. 'But on this occasion you happen to be right. I like my job and I'm good at it. The fact that I am a woman is irrelevant... well, most of the time.'

'Aaah.' He injected a wealth of understanding into the single syllable. 'And those other times?'

Laura sighed, her smile crooked. 'The diplomatic service doesn't know what it's missed. I've gone home after some meetings with my tongue almost bitten in half.'

Brent looked down at her. 'You couldn't hold this job if you weren't capable, so what could possibly provoke such a painful reaction?'

His remark was based on simple logic, yet it ignited a warm glow in the pit of her stomach, and Laura was suddenly wary. To recognise the truth of Brent Lewis's shrewd observations was one thing, but to interpret his remarks as compliments was both foolish and dangerous.

She looked him straight in the eye. 'Patronising men. You see, when discussions are not going their way, they try to cloud the issue.'

'Oh? How?' His curiosity seemed genuine.

'By asking what I'm doing in a job like this instead of fulfilling my natural role as a housewife and mother.'

His expression did not alter. 'And how do you reply?'

At least he hadn't said, 'Well, why *are* you?'

'Usually I just smile, ignore the question, and return to the matter in hand. That's usually sufficient. But now and again there's one who persists. The other day——' she broke off, turning her head to look towards the ship-repair yard at the other side of the harbour. She hadn't meant to let that slip, but the incident still rankled.

'The other day?' Brent prompted.

Laura smiled and shook her head, trying to dismiss the subject. He stepped in front of her, forcing her to stop.

'Come on, you can't leave it there,' he chided. 'The suspense is killing me.'

'Hardly,' Laura flashed him an ironic glance. 'It would take far more to bother you than my refusal to answer a question.'

'That would depend very much on the question,' was his instant response. His deep voice, unexpectedly soft, sent a shiver feathering down Laura's spine. 'But tell me what happened—please.'

There had been a subtle but undeniable change in the atmosphere between them. Brent's coolness and tightly curbed anger, previously so evident, had disappeared, to be replaced by a teasing intimacy, a banter that was gradually, insidiously, gnawing away at her protective shell. Somewhere, far off, Laura caught the echo of a warning, but it grew fainter and was lost.

She took a deep breath. 'The person concerned refused to take the hint. I happen to know he only took up his present post recently. So I asked him whether, at his interview, he had been questioned about his private life. He was obviously startled and said, "Of course not". So I told him I hadn't either and, as my employer did not consider it any of *his* business, I certainly didn't owe explanations to anyone else. I told him his questions were impertinent, irrelevant, and an invasion of privacy to which I took great exception.' She bit her lip as the ghost of a smile lifted the corners of her mouth. 'Though he deserved it, I felt almost sorry for him. He looked *stunned*.'

'I'm not surprised,' Brent murmured. He turned casually towards her. His expression was still one of polite interest, but his eyes were piercing. 'Weren't you engaged the last time we met?'

Automatically Laura stiffened, then forced herself to relax. It was over, past, finished. She had come through it bruised but unbroken and Jeremy was out of her life for good. 'Yes.' Her reply was curt.

Though her reaction had been swiftly controlled, it had not escaped Brent. Had Laura dared meet his eye she would have seen scepticism battling with growing curiosity as he tried to reconcile the deep hurt he saw in her response with the unpleasant insinuations Jeremy Grainger had made at their meeting in Rotterdam a few weeks ago.

He caught her left hand and lifted it, bare of rings, into view. 'I gather you're not any more.'

His touch sent tiny shocks pulsing up her arm and, swiftly, she pulled her hand free. 'That's right.'

There was a pause. 'Good,' he said.

Laura looked at him quickly, but he was gazing around at the activity on the ships and jetties. Then, with a brief smile at her, he turned and began retracing their path back towards the town. Automatically, Laura followed.

'What do you mean, *good*?'

'Well, it saves any complications.'

'What *complications*?'

His smile had a mocking edge and there was a gleam in his eyes that quickened Laura's heartbeat.

'Surely it's obvious?'

'Not to me.'

'You've invited me to lunch. You've promised to introduce me to all the people you think I need to see in order to write my reports. Correct?'

'Yes. It's normal business practice to——'

He did not let her finish. 'So we are going to be spending a great deal of time together, you and I, not all of it in office hours.'

Laura's mouth dried as the words slid smoothly off his tongue. She wanted to argue, to tell him she saw no need for contact outside office hours, but what could she say?

Evening meetings over drinks and dinner were all part of business life. But Dennis had always done the entertaining. He enjoyed it and had a flair for finalising lucrative deals with clients mellowed by good food and wine and his fund of amusing anecdotes. Only Dennis wasn't here, and he was relying on *her*. How could she admit her lack of experience?

'You get my point?' Brent was saying. 'A jealous fiancé, divided loyalties...' he shrugged, leaving the sentence unfinished.

Laura swallowed. 'I know exactly where my loyalties lie, Mr Lewis.'

'Brent,' he corrected softly.

She ignored it. Maybe there was a way out. She could cope with the days. But evenings—that was different. 'I offered my assistance and I don't break my word. However, if you wish to pursue certain lines of enquiry on your own——'

'I wouldn't dream of it,' he interrupted, and beneath the blandness of his reply she heard the ring of cold steel.

Oh Dennis, Laura cried silently, *what have you got me into?* She lifted her chin. 'As you wish. Now that's settled I suggest I introduce you to the captain of the port. His office is just over here.'

Laura was surprised and slightly piqued at the welcome Brent received and the speed with which they were ushered into Captain Lincoln's office. The whole building hummed with activity. Phones rang, type-

writers clattered, doors slammed, s
ranks thronged the corridors while sta
hurried in and out of offices.

Laura listened while the two men talked.
shorthand entries in a small notebook take   is
shirt-pocket. Every few minutes planes roared   head
on their approach to the airport which was built on the
low flat land between the Rock and the Spanish
mainland, and jutted out into the sapphire waters of the
bay.

She tried hard to concentrate on Brent's questions
concerning the requirements of the many different types
of ship using the harbour, and the captain's replies, but
her own thoughts intruded, clamouring for her attention.

She had expected resistance, even a flat refusal on
Brent's part to have her accompany him. Subcon-
sciously she had been gearing herself up to fight, racking
her brain for every conceivable reason he *should* take
her along.

Now the whole situation was suddenly reversed and
she was frantically searching for excuses *not* to spend
every waking hour with him as he evidently intended she
should.

Of course, it was exactly what Dennis had wanted,
and Brent was playing right into their hands.

She risked a glance at him. His head was bent. A lock
of black hair had fallen across his forehead. He sat with
one leg loosely crossed over the other, completely at ease,
and his pen flew over the page as Sam Lincoln outlined
plans for the cruise-liner passenger terminal.

There was no denying his good looks, but his attraction ran deeper than that. He had an incisive mind
and a dry wit, and he had not, as so many others did,
talked *down* to her. All of which surely enhanced the
prospect of working closely with him.

no, it didn't. Because the arrival of Brent Lewis had jolted her with the realisation of how unbalanced her life was.

Laura felt lost, bewildered. Why *him*? She had dealings with relatively few women in her professional life and was quite used to working with men. So why had *he* had that effect?

She would have to maintain distance between Brent and herself, make it crystal clear that the time they spent together, whether in the dock area or at dinner, was solely for business. Maybe that was unnecessary. Perhaps she had imagined the light in his eyes that hinted at a more than professional interest. Even as she told herself there would be no problems, she knew she was lying. Because, after fifteen months of emotional hibernation, she had woken up.

For the first time since finishing with Jeremy over a year ago, she knew herself lonely and longing for the comfort of a man's arms. But the man who had kindled this awareness, who had forced her to face the truth, was a threat. A threat to the professional secrets she was forced to hide, and even more of a threat to her hard-won peace of mind. Yet she was drawn to him, like a moth to flame. He was unlike anyone she had ever met: totally self-contained, with a coolness that bordered on arrogance; and his acute perception unnerved her. Yet she could not forget that brief glimpse of vulnerability. There was far more to Brent Lewis than the façade he presented to the world. But in order to discover what lay behind that façade she would have to take terrible risks. Was she strong enough to take the consequences if it all went wrong *again*?

'Don't you agree, Miss Jefford?'

Laura jumped, switching her gaze to the captain who, smiling, was clearly waiting for an answer.

From the corner of her eye she caught Brent's sardonic grin and felt her colour rise. *He knew what she'd been thinking.* She caught herself. That was ridiculous, impossible. She was careful not to look at him.

'I—I'm so sorry, Captain, I didn't catch what you said.'

'It's the damned planes. I've got used to them, I forget other people haven't. I was just saying I think Mr Lewis will be pretty impressed by the plans for updating all the harbour facilities.'

Laura glanced at Brent. 'I don't see how he could fail to be.' She smiled and stood up. 'I think we've taken enough of your time for now, Captain. I know how busy you are, but as we were in the area it seemed too good an opportunity to miss.'

'Never too busy to see you.' The captain's leathery face cracked into a grin. 'Drilling's almost finished, isn't it? I guess the company will be appointing a project manager soon.' He paused, his blue eyes sharp with curiosity. 'Think you'll get the job? You're virtually doing it now.'

Laura's smile was non-committal. 'We'll see.'

Back in the office, at Brent's request, she unrolled the plans and spread them out on her desk. He came round beside her to study them, leaning forward on one hand.

She remained upright, acutely aware of his body warmth. He smelled of soap and a tangy aftershave. His thick hair gleamed with health and his broad shoulders strained the olive cotton of his shirt.

She had an overpowering urge to reach out and touch him, to feel the texture of his bronzed skin and the roughness of the dark hair on his forearms. Yet, at the same time, the idea petrified her. To travel that path meant pain. She had loved a man once and it had almost destroyed her. Why should it be different a second time?

What was happening to her? Why was she thinking this way?

Without looking up, Brent began to question her about various points on the plans.

Moistening her lips, she answered clearly and concisely, vastly grateful for the interruption of her wild and wayward thoughts.

After a few minutes he straightened up and, facing her, folded his arms. 'Off the record, do you think you'll get the project manager's job?'

Lowering her eyes, Laura shrugged. 'That's not for me to say.'

'Of course it is,' he retorted impatiently. 'Would you *like* it?'

She looked up at him. 'Off the record?' He nodded. 'Yes, I would. I've been involved right from the beginning, even before I came out here. I'd love the opportunity to see the project through to completion.'

He tilted his head, observing her through narrowed eyes. 'Would you describe yourself as ambitious?'

'I—I don't—I'm not really sure. I enjoy a challenge and I like to finish what I start.'

'I'll keep that in mind,' he murmured, holding her gaze and she felt heat flood her cheeks. 'But you're not a top-of-the-tree-at-any-price woman?'

She shook her head. 'I'm doing quite nicely on my little twig.'

'Don't underestimate yourself,' he said suddenly.

Laura's eyes widened. That was the last thing she had expected to hear, especially from him. 'I don't think I do,' she replied, then blurted, 'Look, what is this? You said "off the record". It's company policy never to give personal interviews. I'll help you in any way I can regarding the project, but I'd prefer you didn't make a big thing out of me or my job. And you did say you wanted to save time, so hadn't we better get on?'

His smile had a bitter edge. 'It's a rare woman who doesn't jump at the opportunity to talk about herself. But then I don't think I've come across anyone quite like you before. You can still blush, for a start.'

Her cheeks on fire, Laura withdrew into herself like a sea-anemone prodded by a careless finger. She turned away and began to roll up the plans. It wasn't *what* he had said. In its own way that had been a compliment. But the way he had said it had been cruel and mocking. She swallowed hard and kept her voice devoid of expression.

'Where would you like to go now?'

'You promised to take me to lunch.'

'Do you prefer any particular type of food?' Laura asked with exquisite politeness. 'We can offer French, Italian, Chinese, Spanish...'

'You're supposed to be showing me round,' he pointed out. 'You choose.' When she did not immediately reply, he added, 'You just said you like a challenge.'

The static was there once more, invisible sparks flashing between them. Laura returned the plans to the top of the filing-cabinet. You're not a challenge, she thought with uncharacteristic vehemence, you're bloody impossible.

She picked up her bag and smiled brightly. 'I know just the place.'

The white-painted cable-car with its red logo clanked over the three supporting towers and came to rest at the Top Station, a thousand feet above the sparkling sea. Absorbed in the magnificent view of which she never tired, Laura was oblivious to Brent's eyes on her and the perplexity that softened the harshness of his features.

She looked at him over her shoulder, her face alight. 'Isn't it fantastic?'

He nodded, not taking his eyes off her. 'Beautiful,' he murmured.

They followed the other two couples out of the car. 'Those people who got out lower down,' Brent said, 'where were they going?'

'To look at the apes, I expect,' Laura replied. 'They roam free over that part of the Rock. Actually, they're not really apes at all.' It was a welcome relief to have the conversation on a totally impersonal topic. 'They're tailless monkeys. Their ancestors are believed to have come over with the first Moorish settlers.'

Even as she mentioned the Moors, her mind replayed the brief but vivid image of Brent Lewis in the robes of Tarik ibn Ziad, his bronzed face a cruel mask as his hooded eyes glittered with a cold fury that chilled her soul. The vision shook her deeply and, despite the warmth of the sun, she shivered.

Desperate to blot it out, she strove for normality. 'Which would you prefer, the self-service restaurant, or the English pub?'

'Whichever has a terrace where we can sit outside. This view is too good to waste.'

Seated at a round white table shaded by an umbrella whose edges stirred gently in the warm breeze, Laura gazed across the straits to the coast of North Africa only fourteen miles away. Naval and merchant ships moved with slow majesty between the Mediterranean and the Atlantic Ocean. Below, in the bay, two cruise liners lay at anchor, their superstructure gleaming white in the sun. A large passenger aircraft curved round on its approach to the airport.

Down in the city people were busy. In shops and offices business was being transacted. Tourists thronged

Main Street, taking advantage of the low prices to buy from the incredible variety of goods: eastern jade and saris, perfume, jewellery, Japanese hi-fi systems and Moroccan leather.

Laura felt strangely detached from it all. She was in a kind of limbo, poised on the brink of changes that were as frightening as they were inevitable.

The sound of footsteps made her glance round and she saw Brent approaching carrying a glass of white wine and a half-pint of beer. He sat down opposite her and raised his mug.

'Would you care to propose a toast?'

Laura picked up her glass, turning it round in her fingers. There were many wishes she could make, but her mind was in such turmoil and her feelings so contradictory she didn't know which to choose. To cover her confusion she took refuge in formality. 'To your stay in Gibraltar. I hope you enjoy it.' She hesitated, then raised the wine to her lips.

Brent gazed at her over the rim of his glass, and what she saw in his bitter-chocolate eyes made her breath catch in her throat. 'I rarely mix business with pleasure,' he said softly. 'But in this case it's unavoidable.'

While they ate, Brent asked her more questions about the Rock's history. Then, as they lingered over a second drink, he turned the conversation back to business. He had already prepared a list of the people he wanted to talk to and, with gentle prompting, persuaded Laura to detail the personalities and working methods of those concerned.

It was almost three when they set off on the return journey.

'We can go back by cable-car,' Laura said, 'or we can, if you'd like, go down the Mediterranean steps. There are some incredible views and the wild flowers are really spectacular. There are lots of birds here at the moment, some of them quite rare. The migrating flights——'

'What I would like,' he interrupted with deceptive gentleness, 'is to go to bed.' Laura froze. There was a pause which, thinking about it later, she was convinced had been deliberate, then he added, 'I'm still slightly jet-lagged.'

'Oh,' she said quickly, 'yes. Of course.' Relief surged through her. She would call in at the office, check with Lisa that nothing urgent had cropped up then, after a walk and perhaps a swim, she would have an early night herself.

For once the thought of being alone was truly inviting. She needed time to think, to come to terms with all that was happening. Time to try and work out how best to deal with the inevitable pressures of working with this unpredictable man.

A moment later her plans lay in fragments.

'After a few hours' sleep and a hot shower I'll be ready to see what nightlife this place has to offer. Where are you staying?'

Laura stared at him. 'I—why?'

'I need to know where to pick you up,' he said with exaggerated patience. 'By the way, dinner is on me tonight. That way I can at least be sure we get a decent meal.'

'Listen,' Laura retorted hotly, 'I offered you the choice. We could have gone anywhere you wanted.'

'I wanted to know what *you* would choose, and I learned that food is less important to you than the surroundings. Now I like salad, but I've travelled several thousand miles in the last few days and I need something more substantial if I'm to function efficiently.'

'Then perhaps I'm the wrong dinner companion,' Laura began crisply.

'On the contrary, I can't imagine anyone more suitable.'

Wondering what he meant, Laura began to shake her head. 'I don't think——'

'Oh, but *I* do,' he cut in smoothly. 'And what I think is that your boss would be very disappointed if he knew you were neglecting me the moment his back was turned. He was there when you told me that *no company with any sense would have more important things to do.* You haven't forgotten, have you?'

'No,' Laura said through gritted teeth, 'I haven't forgotten.'

'So, are you in a hotel? Do you have an apartment, or what?'

She cleared her throat. 'I live at the Holiday Inn.'

He smiled, a slow lazy smile that made her scalp tingle. 'Well, how about that? I'm staying there too. Come on, here's the cable-car.'

Laura looped the pearl rope around her neck, clipped on matching earrings and stood back to check as much of her reflection as she could see in the mirror.

She had chosen a dress of crêpe de Chine in a white, mint and peach print. The bodice, with its slash neckline and three-quarter dolman sleeves bloused softly over a tailored belt. The slim skirt was slit up the back.

Her hair was piled up in a slightly softer style than usual, allowing curling tendrils to frame her face.

To counteract her nervous pallor, she had applied a little extra make-up, and was reassured by the vision of cool elegance that gazed back at her.

Sliding her feet into high-heeled white sandals, Laura picked up her matching clutch-bag and checked its contents.

The phone beside her bed buzzed. She lifted the receiver.

'Are you on your way, or do I come and fetch you?' Brent's deep voice echoed in her ear.

'I'm just coming.' The lightness of her tone was belied by the way her heart pounded against her ribs. This was the first time she had been out to dinner with a man since Jeremy. And it had to be *this* man. 'Anyway, you're early.'

'Correction. You are two minutes late. By the way, what colour is your dress?'

'It's a woman's prerogative,' she countered, never having been late in her life. 'It's mainly white, but has touches of pale green and peach.' She would *not* ask why he wanted to know now when he would shortly see for himself.

'Five minutes is acceptable,' he agreed, 'but longer than that is either bad planning or bad manners.'

'Or inconvenient phone calls,' Laura retorted, and replaced the receiver before he had a chance to reply.

She took one last look in the mirror. The exchange had charged her system with adrenalin. Her cheeks were flushed, her eyes sparkled, and she felt like jelly inside.

As she stepped out of the lift, Brent turned towards her. The expression on his face flooded her body with tingling warmth.

They moved towards one another across the reception area and for a moment, as far as Laura was concerned, the rest of the world ceased to exist.

He wore a fawn light-weight suit and his hair was still damp from the shower.

Laura tilted her chin a fraction higher to mask her uncertainty as his narrowed gaze raked her from head to toe.

He nodded briefly. 'It was worth the wait.' Then he raised the hand he had kept partially hidden behind his back and presented her with a rose. The half-opened petals were creamy-white and tipped with the faintest blush of peach. The stem was sealed inside a slender vial with a pin attached so that the flower could be either worn or carried.

'Oh, it's gorgeous.' She looked up, smiling in unfeigned delight. 'I've never had a corsage before. It reminds me of those lovely, romantic old films.'

She bit her lip and quickly lowered her gaze to the bloom again, inhaling its perfume. Why on earth had she said that? Because it was true. But true or not, it had been a foolish mistake. The last thing she wanted was for him to think that what was probably no more than a pleasant gesture was liable to have its importance wildly exaggerated.

He took the rose from her and opened the pin. 'Do you remember *Intermezzo*?'

She watched his fingers as though hypnotised. 'Wasn't—er—didn't it have Ingrid Bergman and Cary Grant in it? One of them was a concert pianist?'

He nodded. 'I must have seen that film at least five times. It was marvellous. Don't move or one of us will get damaged.'

Laura didn't even breathe as he pinned the rose to her dress just below her left shoulder. She could feel his warm breath on her forehead and was horribly aware of the fire in her cheeks. She stared fixedly at his cream shirt and brown striped tie. His fingers moved with gentle assurance while hers, white-knuckled, gripped her bag ever more tightly as she began to tremble.

'There.' He lowered his hands. One brushed her shoulder and she flinched. As though magnetised, they swayed fractionally towards one another then he stepped back.

'Thank you,' Laura managed. It was only then, glancing up, that she saw the film of sweat on his upper lip and the swiftly suppressed hunger in his glittering eyes.

'Let's go,' he said abruptly and, cupping her elbow, guided her towards the door. She glanced once more at the rose and her heart gave an extra beat.

The seafood meal at the little trattoria was delicious and the light dry wine had smoothed away all the jagged edges caused by the extra stress of the past two days. Laura was enjoying herself more than she would have believed possible as she listened to him describe the many places to which his work had taken him. When he announced that he had talked enough and it was her turn, her stomach had turned over and she had experienced a moment's numbing dread. But he had asked only about her writing and his interest had seemed so real, she had surprised herself, revealing without any evasion the difficulties she was encountering. Yet it was his profession, so surely he, better than anyone else, would understand the problems facing a relative beginner.

It was after ten when they left the restaurant.

'It's been a *lovely* evening,' Laura sighed happily, smiling up at him, totally unaware of how desirable she looked, her eyes shining, her face rosy, and all signs of tension smoothed away.

A muscle jumped in Brent's jaw as he placed a casual arm around her shoulders. 'It's not over yet. Come on, I'll take you dancing.'

'No, thanks all the same, but——'

Brent frowned, clearly puzzled. 'But from what you said I got the impression you spent just about all your nights off in nightclubs and discos.'

'I'm sure I didn't—perhaps I exaggerated, just a little.' She stifled a giggle. 'Actually,' she confided recklessly, 'I'm not a very good dancer at all. No practise, you see. I can only do the slow ones. They give me time to think.'

He looked down at her, his expression unreadable. 'Are you very tired?'

'No——' she began uncertainly.

'Then I know just the place.'

As he turned to wave down a passing taxi, Laura opened her mouth, then shut it again. It *had* been a wonderful evening, relaxed, interesting, and full of fascinating insight into his work. She didn't want it to end, but nor did she want anything to spoil it. They had just spent two hours together without a single spark flying. Wasn't it tempting fate to think the truce could last? Wouldn't it be wiser to part before anything could go wrong and spoil it all?

'Don't look so worried,' he scolded softly, opening the car door. 'I promise you won't be sorry.'

After a moment's hesitation Laura climbed into the taxi. Brent spoke briefly to the driver then climbed in after her, making no attempt to touch her during the short drive.

When the taxi pulled up he got out first and held the door for her.

The driver switched on his transistor, lit a cigarette and took a folded newspaper from the glove compartment, clearly prepared for a wait.

'Come on,' Brent caught her hand in his and walked to the edge of the road.

'Here?' Laura asked.

He looked down at her. 'Disappointed?'

She looked down the wide beach. A full moon hung low over the sea, casting a shimmering path and turning the sand to silver. Above them in the velvet sky, stars hung so bright and low they seemed almost within reach. The night air was as soft as breath and rippled over Laura's flushed face like cool silk.

Small waves broke with a shushing sound on the firm sand and the cries of the nightbirds mingled with the soft whirring of wings as another migrating flock passed overhead.

Impulsively she squeezed his hand. 'Oh, no.'

They stood quite still for a moment, absorbing the peace. The sounds of the city were faint and from the open windows of the taxi Laura could hear a plaintive Spanish ballad.

Letting go of Brent's hand, she bent down, tugged off her shoes and, leaving them on the low wall, started down towards the water.

'Where are you going?' Brent sounded surprised.

'For a paddle,' she called over her shoulder.

He began to laugh. 'Are you mad?'

She paused, frowning thoughtfully. 'No. I think it's an eminently sensible thing to do.'

A few moments later she heard the thud of running footsteps and as he caught her hand once more she saw that not only had he discarded shoes and socks, he had also rolled his trousers half-way up his calves. His hair had flopped over his forehead and his mouth was twisted in a lopsided grin. 'If you can't beat 'em...' he shrugged.

They walked in silence along the water's edge. A slight shift in the wind carried the sound of music towards them. Laura knew the tune well. It had a pulsing rhythm and a haunting melody that had stirred her deeply the first time she heard it.

She was about to mention it to Brent when, laughing softly, he pulled her round to face him and taking her in his arms began to dance with her.

Her feet seemed to have wings. She moved without conscious thought, her body in perfect harmony with his as they whirled and swayed. She glanced over his shoulder and saw in the bright moonlight, two sets of footprints etched on the sea-darkened sand.

Abruptly Brent stopped. His smile faded. With a sound that was almost a groan, he brought his head down and, before Laura realised what was happening, his mouth was on hers.

CHAPTER FOUR

LAURA finished her coffee and stood up to leave. She had come down early hoping to avoid Brent. So far she had succeeded, but it would be foolish to linger.

It had occurred to her to order breakfast in her room, but as she had never done so before, Inez might assume she was ill. If she said she wasn't, there would inevitably be speculation as to the reason for this sudden change in routine, and that was the last thing she wanted.

As she reached the lift the doors opened and there he stood, alone and devastatingly attractive in a light grey suit.

Laura felt as if all the breath had been squeezed out of her.

He recovered first. 'Good morning.' Though his tone was pleasant, his eyes were immediately guarded, avoiding hers, his mouth unsmiling.

'Good morning,' she replied politely, and started past him into the lift.

'What time is our appointment with the Minister of Trade?' he enquired, checking his watch.

Laura's throat was tight as she answered, 'Ten thirty.'

'I'll pick you up from the office at ten fifteen.'

She nodded without speaking and stepped into the empty lift. As she turned, he was already walking away, his loose-limbed stride taking him swiftly across the marble foyer without a backward glance.

Laura blinked hard and stabbed the button.

Soon after Josefa had left, carrying the bundle of files and correspondence Laura had dealt with on Dennis's behalf, Lisa put her head round the door. 'Are you ready to go through your post now? You could leave it till later, *if* you're coming back, that is.' She gave a conspiratorial grin and sighed. 'Some people have all the luck.'

Laura got up from her desk and went to the filing cabinet, keeping her head averted, furious at the sudden tears blinding her. 'Just leave it in the tray, please. I'll buzz when I'm ready.'

'Oh, OK.' Clearly surprised by the abrupt dismissal, Lisa did as she was asked and went out again.

Motionless, her hands resting on the edge of the drawer, Laura could hear the soft murmur of female voices through the closed door. No doubt Lisa was asking Josefa if *she* had noticed anything odd.

Slamming the drawer shut, Laura folded her arms and stared out of the window, oblivious of the sunny morning.

She was back on the beach, in Brent's arms, his mouth on hers. She had never been kissed like that before. Full of hunger, yearning and need, it had melted her bones and left her light-headed and shaken. When at last his lips had reluctantly left hers, they had clung to one another, stunned and breathless.

Defenceless, her protective shell shattered beyond repair, she had stared into his face. In the bright moonlight she had watched in disbelief his gaze harden, becoming opaque, shutting her out as firmly as his hands gripping her upper arms had set her apart from him.

Tentatively she had smiled, tried to make a joke, but his expression had remained stony and he had not responded.

They had returned to the taxi, Brent distant, uncommunicative, and herself bewildered and achingly lonely. She longed to ask him *why*. What had gone wrong? It had felt so good, so *right*. But glancing at the dark, silent man beside her, her courage failed. During the ride she told herself it didn't matter, it wasn't important. *It was only a kiss.*

Back at the hotel, he had insisted on escorting her to her door. Hope had surged. Maybe he would explain, maybe they would talk. But as soon as she had turned the key and opened it, he had muttered 'goodnight' and walked away down the corridor, leaving her staring after him, hopelessly confused, angry, and certain she had made a complete fool of herself.

She had slept little that night, tossing and turning, going over the evening again and again in her mind, trying to work out what had gone wrong.

For her it had been wonderful. From the moment he had given her the rose, the evening had assumed a magical quality. As they danced on the moonlit sand to the accompaniment of wind and waves, it had all seemed perfect. And when he had kissed her...Laura's eyes closed and a shaft of exquisite sweetness pierced her as she relived an ecstasy she had never known before.

He had been as deeply affected as she had, she would stake her life on it. Then he had retreated behind an impenetrable barrier. *Why?*

The intercom buzzed. Turning from the window, Laura leaned over her desk and pressed the switch. 'Yes, Lisa?'

'Mr Ansaldo's secretary for you.'

'Thank you. Put her through.' Laura picked up the phone and sat down in her swivel chair. 'Good morning.' She listened for a few moments. 'No, of course I understand. Yes, eleven thirty will be fine. Goodbye.' She replaced the receiver and sighed.

The door opened and Brent walked in. 'Ready?'

Laura stood up. She felt more in control on her feet, less vulnerable. 'I—I'm afraid we can't go yet. I've just had a phone call from the minister's secretary. He's been delayed at an important meeting at the Convent.'

Brent's eyebrows rose and Laura explained. 'The Convent is the Governor's residence.'

'Don't the nuns mind sharing?' Brent enquired.

Not sure whether he was joking, Laura decided to play safe, and shook her head. 'I don't think any nuns have ever lived there. The word "convent" is a bit confusing, it doesn't have quite the same meaning here.'

'Really?' Both his voice and face were devoid of expression. 'What does it mean?'

'It is, or rather was, a religious house,' Laura explained, 'but in Spain while the home of a totally enclosed order is called a monastery, monks who go out into the world, like the Franciscan Friars, call their home a convent. It was the Friars who built the convent in 1531. It became the Governor's residence in the early 1700s.'

'You certainly know your history,' he observed, his gaze travelling the room.

She shrugged, not feeling the least bit casual. 'All part of the service.'

'Is our appointment cancelled or simply postponed?'

'His secretary suggested eleven thirty instead. I accepted.'

'Fine.' Brent looked at his watch. He seemed oddly restless. Laura had the impression of a coiled spring, tightly controlled. 'That gives us just over an hour. Not long enough to go out and do anything worthwhile.' He paused. 'I suggest we use the time to go over the rest of the details concerning Phoenix's ro-ro berth.' He lowered himself into the chair Josefa had recently occupied.

'Fine,' Laura echoed faintly and resumed her own seat. Neither of them had time to *waste*, but he was behaving as though last night had never happened. Perhaps she had dreamed it. Maybe the whole wonderful three and a half hours had been a figment of her imagination, a splurge of wishful thinking.

Then she remembered the rose, now in a crystal vase on her bedside table, its sweet perfume scenting the room. She hadn't imagined that. Or his kiss. Her powers of invention simply weren't that strong.

But whatever his reasons, if he wanted the whole matter forgotten, she would be the last person to remind him. Pride kept the head high. All the disillusion and raw hurt were hidden inside.

'Do you want to see the plans again?' She started to get up, marvelling at her own acting ability. She sounded so cool, so detached.

'No.' He was abrupt, raising his hand to make her stay where she was. 'Not just now.'

Their eyes met for the first time since he had entered the room. The contact was brief, lasting barely a second before he turned his head, reaching into his inside pocket for notebook and pen.

Heat coursed through her and she busied herself sorting through the files, seared by what she had seen. *He had not forgotten.* The memory was there, vivid, burning bright in his gaze. Her heart thudded so loudly it deafened her.

'Er—give me a run-down on the projected timing of stages from now to the berth being in operation,' he demanded brusquely.

Instead of being angered by his tone and responding immediately in kind, she simply nodded as the knowledge that what had occurred between them the previous night was far from over seeped, heady and dangerous, along her veins.

Laura swallowed. 'Yes, of course.' She was just explaining Gibraltar's need for a berth where lorries carrying general cargo to and from foreign ports could simply drive on and drive off carrier-ships, saving time and handling charges, when the intercom buzzed again.

'Mr Sanderson for you.'

'Den——?' Laura bit the name off and darted a glance at Brent who appeared to be checking his notes. Why was Dennis phoning? He'd only been gone a couple of days. The bank meeting, it had to be. Mentally she crossed her fingers. *Let it be good news.* Even so, with Brent Lewis sitting barely two feet away, she would have to watch what she said. 'Put him on, Lisa, and bring in some coffee would you, please?'

There was a pause and several clicks on the line. 'Hello? Dennis? I thought you were supposed to be on holiday.'

Dennis's voice came clearly down the line and Laura pressed the receiver more closely to her ear. 'Everything all right there, Laura?'

'Fine,' she replied brightly. 'Mr Lewis is here with me. We're just going over the project schedule before our meeting with Mr Ansaldo. Are Margaret and the girls well?'

'Margaret's with me now.' Dennis sounded strained. 'Listen, Laura, I've only got a minute. I spent two hours with our merchant bankers yesterday morning. I really laid it on the line, but they wouldn't give me an immediate decision. They'll be contacting you within the next couple of days.'

Laura gripped the phone more tightly. 'I don't understand. Why me? If you've——'

Dennis cut in, 'Sorry, Laura, I've got to go. Margaret will explain. Good luck, girl. I'm relying on you.'

Involuntarily Laura's voice sharpened. 'Dennis? Wait, I——' There was a confusion of noises at the other end, then Margaret's soft Welsh lilt.

'Laura? Still there are you?'

Mindful of Brent's presence, Laura clamped down on the apprehension welling up inside her. 'Yes.'

'Listen, love, we're calling from the hospital. Dennis is being operated on this afternoon.'

Brent's head jerked up at her shocked exclamation. *'What?'* Laura abandoned all pretence. 'What is it? What's happened?'

'A perforated ulcer. At least they're pretty certain that's what it is.' Margaret's voice wobbled. 'He collapsed yesterday afternoon when he got home from the meeting in London.'

'Oh, Margaret, I'm so sorry.'

'Yes, well…' Dennis's wife cleared her throat and tried to disguise her own shock and worry behind a brisk matter-of-factness. 'He's in the best place and the doctors have been marvellous. But they've warned him he'll be in here at least a fortnight, and then he'll have to convalesce for a while.'

'I'm sure he couldn't be in better hands.' Laura tried to offer comfort, refusing to think for the moment about where this development left her. 'And Margaret, tell him not to worry, everything is under control here.' Professionally, at least, that was true.

'I told him you'd be all right. "Laura will manage," I said. Those were my very words.'

Laura tried to smile. 'Didn't I have the best teacher?'

'I must go, love. They're moving him to another ward and he'll only fret if I'm not there. He hates hospitals, see. 'Bye now.'

'Goodbye, Margaret.' But the line was already dead. As Laura slowly replaced the phone, Lisa walked in with a tray.

Brent was on his feet in an instant. He took it from her, the warmth of his smile making the secretary all dewy-eyed. 'Thank you, Lisa. I'll see to it.'

Lisa darted a curious glance at Laura who was staring blankly at the phone. 'You sure? It's no trouble.'

'Quite sure.' Brent was still smiling, but his tone was firm. 'I expect you have lots to do.'

'Yes, well...' Lisa backed towards the door, clearly dying to know what was going on, and why her boss, who *always* had time for a few moments' chat at coffee time or between appointments, had suddenly become so uncommunicative.

'Miss Jefford will call when she wants you,' Brent said, and Lisa was sharp enough to realise he meant that until she was summoned she was to stay out. Before she could reply he had closed the door.

'Has there been an accident?' he asked gently as he began pouring the coffee. 'Cream and sugar, isn't it?'

She nodded, part of her mind registering with surprise the fact that he had remembered her tastes. 'Not an accident, no. Perforated ulcer.'

'Nasty.' Frowning, Brent leaned forward to place the cup in front of her. 'But he must have had some warning. Why didn't he get treatment before it reached this stage?'

Unable to sit still, Laura pushed back her chair and went to the window. Her back to Brent, she rubbed her arms through the jacket of her primrose linen suit. The same thought had been gnawing at her. She recalled Dennis's complaint of indigestion, the pain below his breastbone shrugged off, the sudden sweaty greyness either ignored or blamed on faulty air-conditioning. She thought also of the pressure he had been under, from

the Minister, the merchant bank, the port authority and
all the other groups and individuals for and against the
development. They had been ranged on one side and the
group's executive board on the other. Dennis had been
performing the business equivalent of a juggling act on
a tightrope. One slip, one lapse in concentration, and
the whole lot might have come tumbling down. She had
done what she could, but the final responsibility had
been his.

'Sorry,' Brent said quietly. 'That was a stupid thing
to say. It's always easy to be wise *after* the event, to
point out all the things one *should* have done. Obviously
he must have been under a lot of pressure or he would
have noticed the warning signs and done something about
them.'

Laura froze. She didn't dare turn around. Maybe Brent
was just being sympathetic. There was no denying the
warmth in his tone. But once he realised the deeper truth
in what he had just said, that a man would have to be
under enormous mental stress to be able to ignore
physical pain, he would start digging deeper. He would
have to, it was his job. *And hers, at all costs, was to
stop him.*

She heard his chair move, and his footsteps. She sensed
him behind her. She closed her eyes. His hands were
gentle on her shoulders, but his touch made her weak
inside.

'You've had a shock. Come and drink your coffee.
You'll feel better.'

He sounded so warm and sympathetic. How she
longed to lean back, to draw strength from him. But
only minutes ago he had been cold and distant, keeping
her physically and emotionally at arm's length. Was this
sudden change genuine, an acknowledgement of last
night? Or had the journalist scented a story?

No. She didn't want to think like that. But could she afford not to?

'Laura? Are you all right?' There was no doubting his concern.

She nodded, forcing herself to smile as he turned her round. 'It's just a lot to take in.' She moved her shoulders awkwardly.

His fingers dug into her arms. Her smile faded as she stood helpless in his grasp. 'Laura,' he searched her face. 'Laura, I——' Compressing his lips he released her, clenching his fists. He half turned away, running one hand, with barely controlled violence, through his hair. 'It would be an impertinence to offer you any help,' he said, staring at the floor. 'But if there *is* anything I can do,' he glanced up at her, his face set, 'promise me you'll ask?'

'Thank you,' Laura replied politely and started towards her desk. But he caught her chin, forcing her to meet his gaze.

'Promise me,' he demanded. The current arced between them.

'I promise,' Laura whispered.

She sipped her coffee, cradling her cup, warming hands which, despite the warm spring sunshine, were cold.

Brent leaned back in his chair. 'Does this mean you'll be left in sole charge?'

Laura grimaced. 'I was just wondering the same thing. No doubt Head Office will be in touch within the next day or so.'

'Does the project really need two people at this stage?'

She felt herself tense. 'What exactly are you implying? That if Dennis hadn't been taken ill I wouldn't be necessary?'

'Far from it.' He eyed her shrewdly. 'In the brief time we've worked together I've seen enough to recognise that apart from whatever else you do, your skill in public relations alone makes you extremely valuable to Phoenix. But as your boss had more or less handed you over to me for the duration of my stay, he must have felt you could be spared.'

There was no way Laura could argue without betraying the fact that Dennis's motives were not quite what Brent imagined. She replaced her cup on the tray, admitting, 'We're at a transition stage. The preliminary work is just about complete. We should begin construction in a couple of weeks.'

'Well then, I'd better make the most of you while I've got the chance.' The lightness in his tone was not reflected in his eyes. 'Come on, we don't want to be late for Mr Ansaldo.'

'I—I'll follow you down. I—er—just want to powder my nose.' She watched his tall figure disappear through the outer door then pressed the intercom switch. 'Lisa, will you come in please, and ask Josefa to come with you.'

Checking her appearance in her compact mirror, Laura quickly freshened her lipstick and tucked a wayward tendril into the heavy coil with fingers that trembled as his words echoed and re-echoed in her head.

The two secretaries entered, and Lisa went to pick up the tray.

'Leave that a moment.' Laura explained about Dennis's sudden illness. Both girls were shocked and upset.

'I don't know when he'll be back,' she said in answer to Josefa's question. 'So for the time being I'll be doing his work as well as my own. Fortunately, things should be reasonably quiet for the next couple of weeks. Dennis has told me to expect a very important call from London within the next day or two. If I'm out of the office, I'll leave a number where I can be reached, so contact me immediately, OK?'

Both girls nodded, their expressions serious.

'The call is highly confidential,' Laura went on. 'It must not be mentioned outside this office.'

Lisa looked uncertain. 'What about Mr Lewis? Does he count as part of the office?'

Laura felt a peculiar wrench. 'No, he does not,' she said firmly.

After making the introductions, Laura was able to withdraw slightly and allow Brent to conduct his interview with the minister in his own way. It was an education.

Under his subtle questioning, Mr Ansaldo opened up in a way that surprised Laura and, she suspected, would surprise the minister himself when he realised how skilfully he had been drawn on the political as well as the commercial aspects of the port's expansion.

Brent was no suppliant begging for crumbs of information and being dispensed a prepared statement. It was a chess game between two masters, with Brent's determination to have all his questions answered having the edge on the minister's habit of divulging only as much as he decided his listener ought to know.

When they emerged into the sunlight, Laura put on her dark glasses. 'That was quite a grilling you gave him.'

One corner of Brent's mouth lifted. 'He's a politician, they're used to it.'

Laura wasn't so sure, but said nothing.

Brent glanced at his watch. 'What's planned for this afternoon?'

'Nothing,' she answered. 'I wasn't sure what——'

'No problem,' he cut in. 'We'll go back to the hotel and change, then grab some lunch, and you can show me the caves.'

She stared at him.

'What's the matter?'

'N-nothing,' she stammered. 'It's just——' then, clutching at straws, 'I thought you'd be working on your notes.'

'I shall do that tonight. Any other questions?' He didn't wait for her reply. 'Good. Let's go.'

Laura's hesitation was only momentary.

The vast cave formed a natural auditorium. Laura gazed up at the rippling pillars of limestone, their ageless beauty enhanced by coloured lighting. She felt dwarfed by it and automatically lowered her voice. 'I haven't been to a performance, but they have ballets and concerts here sometimes. There is another cave lower down which was discovered during the Second World War. That has an underground lake, but it's not open to the general public.'

'It's odd how a place like this can put things into perspective,' Brent mused.

Laura looked at him. 'How do you mean?'

He pushed both hands into his pockets. 'Those stalagmites were formed by water filtering down through the limestone and carrying particles of dissolved rock with it. The water dripped on to the cave floor leaving the minute speck of rock to harden again. Men discovered fire and the wheel. They moved out of caves and built towns. Wars were fought, civilisations rose and fell, and the water just went on dripping. And this,' he gestured towards the fluted, crenellated columns, giant icicles and petrified streams, 'this is the result.'

'What's it all for? Is that what you're asking?' Laura said tentatively.

He smiled. It was a natural smile, the first she had seen since the previous evening. 'No. What I'm trying to say, and obviously not making myself very clear, is that seeing something like this reminds me of how short life is. Yet we spend so much of it worrying about either the past or the future.' He tilted his head back to look up at the roof.

Laura toyed with the sleeves of the sweater slung around her shoulders. She had changed her linen suit for jeans, trainers and an Indian cotton shirt with the sleeves rolled up. Brent was equally casual in jeans and a sweat-shirt. 'Isn't that perfectly natural? Much of our learning is based on past mistakes—experience,' she corrected quickly. 'And as for the future, without some sort of planning——'

'Yes, I know all about that,' he broke in, turning to face her. 'But don't you see how much time is wasted? The past can't be changed. It has happened, it's fact. But it's over.'

Laura shivered. Hadn't she been trying to convince herself of the very same thing?

'Of course plans are necessary,' he went on, 'but there's no guarantee we'll be around to put them into operation. All that exists, all we can really be sure of, is *now*.' His eyes glittered in the artificial light and as his arm encircled her shoulders and drew her against him, Laura felt a strange weakness in the pit of her stomach.

His lips brushed her temple and the sensation was electric. She started to tilt her head, to seek his mouth with her own, oblivious of the other tourists, oblivious of everything but the longing for his kiss. Even as she felt his arm tighten she could hardly believe it. She had hoped so much, but after the way they had parted, and this morning . . . happiness bubbled up inside her. Then, as though someone had pulled a plug, it drained away.

She stiffened and broke free. *The change had been so sudden.* Last night, after stirring her to the very roots of her being and seeming himself to be equally affected,

he had, without a word of explanation, deliberately and
coldly distanced himself. This morning had, in its own
way, been even worse, *until Dennis's phone call*.

Laura closed her eyes tightly. No. He wouldn't, he
couldn't use the attraction she had made it all too plain
he had for her to worm his way into her confidence and
so find out what problems and pressures were at work
within the company. He couldn't be so cynical. *But he
was a journalist.* Wasn't a degree in cynicism one of the
necessary qualifications? *No.* But the seed of doubt was
growing, strangling her hope.

'Laura?' His deep voice was quiet. She was so immersed in the battle within herself, she didn't hear the
note of uncertainty.

Swinging round, her face taut with strain, she lifted
her chin. 'Live for the moment?' she challenged. 'Is that
what you're saying? Eat, drink and be merry, for tomorrow we die?'

His eyes narrowed. 'Is there something wrong?'

'With that philosophy?' She gave a short harsh laugh.
'Not if you're a man.'

'I mean is there something wrong with you?'

'No, there damn well isn't,' she spat. 'Except perhaps
a foolish desire to believe the best of people. I should
have learned by now——' She choked on the words as
he seized her shoulders.

'What *is* this?' he demanded fiercely. 'What's
happened?'

'Nothing,' she blazed back. 'And it's not going to
either. Now let go of me.'

They glared at each other. Laura's heart hammered
furiously. Brent's fingers were biting cruelly into her
flesh. She would bear the bruises for days. But her rage
and lacerating sense of betrayal kept the pain from
showing in her face.

With a visible effort he fought to control his anger. After several moments he released her, clenching his fists as his hands fell to his sides. He sucked in a deep breath. 'Look, there's been a misunderstanding.'

Laura took a step back, her eyes never leaving his. 'No,' she said with quiet force. 'I understand all too well. I only wish I didn't.' She turned and started towards the entrance, pain stabbing like a knife in her breast.

He caught up with her outside. But her eyes, hot and gritty, were safely shielded from his piercing gaze by her sunglasses.

'Where are you going?' he demanded coolly, voice and expression once more under perfect control.

'Back to the office,' she replied. 'With Dennis away there'll be extra work. I can't afford to let it pile up.'

'So you'd like to withdraw from our arrangement?'

Even as relief washed through her, Laura felt a pang of regret. Of course it was for the best. Whatever dreams she had cherished were just that, dreams. They had no basis in reality. Despite the magnetic attraction between them which, even now after all that had happened, still vibrated below the surface, she had to admit there was no possible future in any kind of relationship, personal or professional. They were just too far apart in the things that mattered. Even he seemed to have recognised that. She hadn't believed it would be so easy.

'Under the circumstances——'

'Forget it,' he said flatly. Shocked, she caught her breath and he went on, 'I don't know which *circumstances* you're referring to, your boss's illness or whatever crossed lines you've got in your head, but the arrangement stands. Naturally I'll make allowances for any extra work you might have——'

'Thank you,' Laura injected bitterly.

'—but Dennis Sanderson seconded you to me,' he went on as though she had not spoken, 'and until I hear otherwise *from him* that's the way it stays.'

'You can't——' Laura began, but got no further.

'Oh yes, I can.' His smile had a razor-edge and his eyes were glacial. 'My reports carry weight in the City. Those were your own words, in Sanderson's hearing.' He fell silent watching as all the implications registered.

'That's blackmail,' she whispered.

'No, just fact. Shall we go and look at the apes on our way down?'

When Laura didn't answer, Brent stood in front of her forcing her to stop. His voice was strangely hoarse. 'Don't fight me, Laura. You can't win.'

Her head jerked up. 'No.' She swallowed the lump in her throat. 'I don't have your weapons. I'm not practised in lying, cheating and deceiving people.'

There was a long silence, broken only by the cries of the birds, the whisper of the wind in the eucalyptus and pine trees bordering the road, the drone of insects among the rock lilies, narcissi and candytuft.

Laura waited for his fury to descend on her. Surely she had goaded him beyond the limits of his self-restraint? Not that she regretted a single word. It was no more than he deserved.

But when it came, his reply left her even more confused. 'Nor am I,' he said quietly. 'I've never found such behaviour necessary. I'm sorry if you have.' Before she could respond he had started off down the road.

As they walked back to the office, his disinclination to talk gave Laura the opportunity for some hard thinking but did nothing to diminish her confusion.

'There were no calls,' Josefa smiled as she handed Laura a sheaf of Telex messages. 'There's one from Head Office in there.'

'Thank you. Lisa, would you make us some tea, please?' Laura led the way into her office.

'Do you know anyone in the Chamber of Commerce?' Brent asked perching on the edge of her desk.

Taking off her glasses, she laid the messages on her blotter. 'I've had dealings with one of the directors,' she said, unable to prevent a mild grimace.

'Ah.' Brent nodded. 'Would I be right in thinking he was the gentleman responsible for your bitten tongue?'

She should have remembered how observant he was. 'You would and he was. But "gentleman" is not exactly the term I'd have chosen to describe him.' Their eyes met and, for the first time in over an hour, neither looked away. There was a moment's hesitation, then one corner of Brent's mouth quivered and Laura felt her own mouth widen in a tentative grin. She shrugged awkwardly. 'I'm surprised you remembered.'

'I don't think there's much about you I'd forget.' His quiet reply was tinged with irony and Laura's cheeks grew pink.

'Would you like me to arrange an appointment for you?'

'For *us*,' he corrected, openly grinning.

Laura was oddly breathless. A truce had been called. She picked up the phone and by the time an appointment had been set up for the following afternoon, Lisa had brought in the tea and, after a lingering smile at Brent, gone again.

Laura sat down behind her desk and picking up the Telex flimsies, began flicking through them. 'Will you excuse me for just a minute? I must see if there's anyth——' She froze, staring at the short paragraph. 'Oh, no,' she whispered, willing it not to be true. Not that, not on top of everything else.

'It's not your boss, is it?' Brent asked, concerned.

'No. Yes.' Laura stuttered. She looked up at him, realising from his sudden frown that the cold sickness
churning her stomach must be visible on her face, but
totally incapable of doing anything about it. She fo-
cused on the paper once more. The impact was scarcely
less the second time. 'It's——' She cleared her throat
and tried again. 'It's from Group Head Office. They've
organised a replacement for Dennis.'

'So soon?' Brent seemed surprised.

'Th—they're very efficient,' Laura's teeth were beginning to chatter as shock took hold.

'I wouldn't have thought it necessary to rush a replacement out quite so fast,' he said thoughtfully.
'Sanderson's reports must have made it clear you are
perfectly capable of running things at least until a decision has been reached about a project manager.'

At any other time Laura would have glowed under the
implied compliment. She barely noticed it. Letting the
flimsy slide through her fingers on to the desk, she held
out a shaking hand for the cup and saucer. 'Apparently
they've managed to solve both problems in one move.'
She clattered the cup down on to the desk and tea slopped
into the saucer. Unable to sit still a moment longer, she
got up and went to the window. The sun was sinking in
the afternoon sky, casting long shadows.

'So, who have they appointed?'

Laura rubbed her arms and moistened dry lips.
'Jeremy Grainger.'

CHAPTER FIVE

THERE was a pause while Brent digested this information. Laura waited tensely. She could almost hear his brain working. He had the memory of a herd of elephants. He would remember and he would ask.

'Weren't you and he——?' Brent left the question hanging.

'We were engaged,' she acknowledged tightly.

'So what happened?'

She swung round. 'I don't think it's any of your business.'

'That's debatable.' He replaced his cup and leaned back. He seemed totally relaxed, but his eyes betrayed him. Slightly hooded, their piercing gaze was that of a bird of prey, bright, alert, missing nothing. 'It could be said that something which has clearly shaken you might conceivably affect your work and thus the company.'

Before she could deny the allegation, even though she had to admit its truth, he leaned forward. 'Laura, you have to tell someone.'

Startled, she stared at him. *How did he know she had kept it all locked up inside her?* He didn't. He couldn't. He was just guessing.

Her tongue snaked out. Her lips were paper-dry. 'Th-there's nothing to tell. It didn't work out, that's all.'

Brent examined the nails on one strong, long-fingered hand. 'I was in Rotterdam a couple of months ago,' he announced.

'Oh?' Laura tried for total lack of interest, and failed. Returning to her desk she resumed her seat.

'I did an interview with Grainger. Funnily enough, he mentioned you.'

'Really.' She could feel the scream building up inside her. *Brent Lewis was relentless.*

'Mmm. It was quite odd. I got the distinct impression he was jealous of you.'

Laura was astounded. *'Jealous?* Of *me*?' Brent nodded. 'But—I don't understand. Why?'

'Management at Rotterdam was *technically* a promotion from his previous position with Phoenix,' Brent explained, 'but in fact it was a shunt sideways as far as further advancement is concerned. At least that's the way I read it, and I've seen plenty of similar situations.' He paused. 'Grainger saw it that way too. By the way, who broke off the engagement?'

Laura swallowed. 'I did.'

Brent whistled softly but, to Laura's heartfelt relief, did not ask why.

She placed her hands flat on the desk. 'I'm going to apply for a transfer.'

It was Brent's turn to look startled. He recovered at once.

'Running away?' He might have been asking if she wanted more tea.

'No,' she flared, 'preventing a situation——'

'Come on,' he cut in brusquely. 'Who are you trying to kid? Whatever you call it, it amounts to the same thing.' His voice roughened. 'Laura, you can't leave now.'

Her chin lifted. 'Oh, no? Give me one good reason why I should stay.'

He was silent, visibly battling with some inner decision.

'Exactly,' she murmured, and reached for the phone.

'Where's your pride?' he grated. 'And what about Dennis Sanderson? Don't you owe it to him to stick this out? So much for loyalty.' His disgust brought a flush to her cheeks, but it was a flush of anger.

Loyalty? Who did he think he was? He had lost his fiancée because of his philandering. What price *his* loyalty? 'What would you know about it?' she cried, then stopped abruptly, realising that if she pursued the subject she would have to admit knowing about Cheryl and Gavin, and until she was *absolutely* certain the girl her brother was marrying was Brent Lewis's ex-fiancée, kindness and common sense dictated she kept quiet.

His dark brows met in a thick, unbroken line and his gaze sharpened.

'You don't work for a company,' she amended hastily. 'Being freelance, you owe allegiance to no one. You have only yourself to consider.' Her heart thumped against her ribs. She pulled the post tray towards her and, barely conscious of what she was doing, began sorting through the day's correspondence and reports.

'I don't see it quite like that,' he said quietly. 'Yes, I'm freelance, but much of my work is commissioned and, as far as I'm concerned, the company paying me is entitled to my loyalty.'

Laura felt a sinking sensation. He could not put it more plainly. He had a job to do. If it meant digging below the surface to get the full story, then he had no choice. But he hadn't finished.

'I'm talking about *professional* loyalty. Say I'm doing an article about a certain company. In the course of my investigations I might pick up all sorts of information. Gossip about personal relationships, financial difficulties, that sort of thing.' Laura's stomach knotted. 'A couple of weeks later I could well be working for a rival organisation to whom that information might be worth a great deal.'

Laura couldn't meet his eyes. 'So, do you pass it on?'

The silence dragged. She looked up, unable to stand the suspense, and saw him shake his head. 'I'm a shipping journalist, not a muck-raker. It's of no concern to me whether the chairman of the board is keeping a harem, so long as he's not embezzling company funds to pay for it. Unless something I learn has a direct bearing on the company's ability to trade, I don't consider it any of my business.'

If the bank didn't come up with the money, Phoenix would not be able to fulfil its commitments. Laura shuddered.

'No wonder you're at the top,' she murmured, recognising the truth of his claim to integrity.

His smile was weary and cynical. 'You mean I've made it because I know enough to blackmail some highly placed people?'

'No,' Laura cried swiftly. 'Because they know you *won't.'*

Brent raised one dark brow. 'You mean they trust me?' He was forcing her into a corner.

Laura hesitated. 'I . . . yes, I suppose they must.'

Unfolding his length from the chair, he bent towards her, arms straight, hands planted on the desk. 'And what about you?' he challenged softly. 'Do you trust me?'

I want to, she thought, *God, how I want to. But I gave Dennis my word.* She tried to smile. 'What a question.'

He did not smile back. 'How about an answer?'

'What . . .' she swallowed, the sound audible, 'what would you do in my place?'

He looked steadily at her for a long moment. Then the creases at the corners of his eyes deepened. *'Touché,'* he murmured, and straightened up. 'I think if I were you, I'd try to get to know me better.'

Laura smothered the hysterical laughter that bubbled inside her. Hadn't she tried that last night, only for him to back off with an abruptness that was like a door slamming in her face?

'So why don't you have dinner with me?'

Laura was torn. Despite last night, despite her promise to Dennis, despite *everything*, she longed to accept. *But* ...

She could not hide her regret. 'I really do have to clear this lot tonight. Anyway, didn't you say earlier that you intended to work on your notes?'

A spasm flickered across his features, leaving them taut and closed. 'You're right,' he said. 'Well, I'll leave you to it. Thanks for the tea.' And he went.

Staring at the closed door, surprised by his acquiescence and swift departure, Laura tried to shake off a sense of loss. With an enormous effort of will, she brought her attention back to the work in front of her.

It was almost nine when she returned to the hotel. The young male receptionist gave her a rather odd smile as he handed over her key.

Half-way across the foyer she hesitated. The sound of soft music, voices, the subdued clink of cutlery drifted up from the restaurant at the bottom of the curving staircase. She walked on to the lift. She wasn't really hungry, she told herself. The truth was she could not face sitting in the restaurant to eat alone, not tonight.

Closing her door, she switched on the lights, tugged off her sweater and tossed it on to the bed. She stood uncertainly in the centre of the room, debating whether to have a quick shower then try to keep her mind occupied by working on another wildlife article, or stretch out and soak in a luxuriously scented bath and confront her thoughts. Her gaze fell on the rose, now fully opened, and her eyes misted as she touched the fragrant petals.

A knock on the door made her jump. Then her face cleared. It was probably Inez with the books she had promised.

She opened the door, a smile of welcome lighting her face. Brent stood in the passage beside a trolley covered with a spotless white cloth on which rested several covered dishes, a bottle of wine, and two glasses. Laura stared at him, momentarily speechless.

'Room service,' he announced blandly.

'B-but I didn't——'

His forehead creased. 'You haven't eaten already?'

'No, but——'

'Nor have I. I've just finished transcribing our interview with the minister. Mind if I bring this in? I'm blocking the passage.' Without waiting for a reply he pushed the trolley past her into the room and guided it to the polished table near the window.

Automatically, Laura closed the door. 'How—how did you know I was back?'

'I bribed one of the receptionists. I was informed the moment you stepped into the lift.'

'But——' She got no further, the words drying in her throat as he turned to face her. He touched her cheek lightly with gentle fingers.

'You weren't going to bother with supper.' It was a statement, not a question.

She lifted one shoulder. 'I'm not hungry.' Even as she spoke, her stomach rumbled and her eyes dipped away. Her body seemed to delight in betraying her.

Brent caught her chin, forcing her to look at him. 'Listen, Laura, you've had one hell of a day, I know that. First there was the news about Sanderson's illness, then Grainger's imminent arrival. But if you hope to stop Grainger establishing himself here permanently, you must pull yourself together.'

Laura stiffened, her immediate reaction anger and resentment. How dare he? Who was he to tell her— But it subsided almost at once. *He was right.* She nodded.

He drew out a chair for her and as she sat down said close to her ear, 'The rose is lasting well.'

It was the first direct reference he had made to the previous night. She felt warm colour creep into her face. 'Yes, it—er—the air-conditioning helps,' she mumbled.

Swiftly, he unloaded the trolley, then uncorked the wine and after filling the two glasses, handed one to her. She had no way of knowing whether the brush of his fingers against hers was accident or design, only that the brief contact made her shiver inside.

He raised his glass, looking deep into her eyes. 'To... trust?' he said softly.

Acknowledging the toast in silence, Laura drank.

As they began to eat, helping each other to the various cold meats and mixed salads, Laura realised just how hungry she was.

With a perception she appreciated, Brent kept the conversation light and impersonal, and very soon she was shaking with laughter as he recounted incidents from his early days as a reporter. Many of the stories were against himself and he told them with a dry humour which made her wonder how she could ever have thought him arrogant.

Under the influence of the food, the wine, the laughter, and the sheer pleasure of his company, she began to relax. But as the tension left her, so the pressures of the day took their toll. Soon her eyelids started to droop and she had to stifle first one yawn, then another.

'It's time I went.' He began to load the dishes back on to the trolley. 'I'm boring you.'

'No,' she cried at once, jerking upright, blinking her eyes wide open. 'No, it's fascinating. I could listen to you talk all night. I love the way you——' She faltered as he glanced sideways and she saw from his expression he had been teasing.

Biting her lip, she got up quickly and went to draw the long curtains. So much for trying to keep her feelings to herself. She should never have had that third glass of wine, it had gone straight to her tongue.

'You certainly have seen life,' she observed, smiling brightly over her shoulder in a frantic effort to disguise her slip. 'Where are you off to next?'

'Hong Kong.'

She was still. Her hands fell from the curtains and she turned to face him. He straightened up.

She had said the first thing that came into her head. But his reply suddenly brought it home to her that he would soon be leaving, that despite the attraction, the clashes, the vividness of their short acquaintanceship, it could not develop into anything stronger.

She should be relieved. After all, it was one pressure less, one thing less to fear or worry about. So why was there a lump in her throat? And why were her eyes prickling? She blinked quickly. It was the wine, making her absurdly emotional.

'Oh,' she nodded, clasping her hands.

He hadn't moved. He simply stood, watching her, his expression unreadable. 'I'm due there in just over three weeks.'

She nodded again, unable to mouth platitudes while her heart was begging him not to go and her head countered that it was better he did, before—*before what?*

He looked at his watch, breaking the spell. 'I'd better let you get some rest.' A muscle jumped at the point of his jaw. He seemed about to say something else but changed his mind.

Kiss me, she pleaded silently.

Abruptly he turned, pushed the trolley to the door, then glanced back, a grin playing at the corners of his mouth. 'Thank you for supper.'

Catching his mood, she tried to smile and waved a careless hand. 'It was no trouble at all. We must do it again sometime.'

As she opened the door for him, he paused, started to speak, changed his mind then, without warning, his dark head swooped down and he pressed a warm, lingering kiss to her parted lips. 'Count on it, Laura,' he said softly. 'Goodnight.'

When she awoke the following morning after the best night's sleep she had had for ages, Laura smiled and sighed deeply as she looked at the rose. Her smile turned to a gasp as she realised she had overslept. She bounded out of bed and raced into the bathroom.

As the lift took her down to the foyer she was still anchoring her thick hair with extra pins.

'Morning off?' Inez queried with a smile.

'Overslept,' Laura grimaced as she slapped her key down on the counter.

Inez's smile faded to concern. 'What about breakfast?' She herself never started work, regardless of which shift she was on, without a substantial meal inside her. How could one maintain one's energy and concentration without proper and adequate fuel?

At first glance, glowing from the shower and her rush to get ready, Laura looked exceptionally pretty. But the smart elegance of her grey and red dress could not disguise the slenderness of her figure. Nor did her skilful make-up entirely hide the shadows like purple thumbprints, beneath her eyes.

'Breakfast? No time. I'll have some coffee as soon as I get to the office.'

'Laura——' Inez warned.

'I know, I know. See you later.' She hurried down the wide steps, high heels clicking, and waved at a taxi which had just delivered another party of tourists from the airport.

'Good morning,' she smiled at the two secretaries as she walked into the outer office. 'Did either of you catch the forecast? It looks pretty black out there.'

'I think it's supposed to clear by lunch time,' Lisa offered, looking up from sorting and opening the morning post.

'Miss Jefford——' Josefa began, but Laura, her mind racing ahead to all the things she had to do that day, cut across.

'No call from London?'

'No, but——'

'Right, well, I'll be here for the rest of the morning. This afternoon Mr Lewis...' Even saying his name gave her a little thrill and she laughed at herself even as she winced at the thought that all too soon he would be gone. 'Mr Lewis and I have an appointment at the Chamber of Commerce. I'll leave instructions that I'm to be told at once should you ring.' She started towards her own office, saying over her shoulder, 'Lisa, be an angel and make me some coffee. I didn't have time for any this morning. Josefa, bring in the post as soon as you're ready.'

'Miss Jefford——' Josefa began again, but as Laura glanced back, her attention was caught by Dennis's door opening to reveal an unpleasantly familiar figure. 'Mr Grainger has arrived,' Josefa finished.

Even though she had known he was coming and had had time to prepare herself, even though she thought she was ready, the sight of Jeremy had the impact of a kick in the stomach.

Clad in an impeccably tailored suit, which gave his shoulders the suggestion of a breadth they did not, in fact, possess, a silk shirt and club tie, he looked much older than she remembered. His immaculately coiffeured corn-coloured hair still lay in crisp, regular waves. His tan, the result of weekly sessions with a sun-lamp, was as rich as ever. But there was a puffiness round his eyes and a softness at his jaw. His mouth, in repose, had a petulant droop at the corners. With the light behind him Laura found it impossible to read his expression.

For an instant neither of them moved. He recovered a fraction ahead of her.

'My *dear* Laura,' he came forward, arms extended. 'How marvellous to see you again.'

She had the presence of mind to stick her hand out for him to shake, thus avoiding his intended kiss on both cheeks. He had always been a great one for Gallic gestures, despite purporting to despise the French for their excitability.

'You're looking wonderful.' He sounded surprised, and stood back, still holding her hand, his gaze sweeping her from head to toe. 'I'm so glad there's nothing wrong. I was just beginning to wonder.'

Laura retrieved her hand and felt her nerves tighten. 'Wrong, Jeremy?' She put on a puzzled expression. 'What could possibly be wrong?'

He looked with heavy meaning at his Rolex Oyster, the gold expanding strap encircling his bony wrist close to his hand where it would be in permanent view, then smiled in understanding. 'Oh, I *see*. You *always* start at this time.'

'No,' she said evenly. 'I'm usually here by eight-thirty, but I worked late last night and didn't leave until nine.'

'I suppose you're finding it a bit difficult to cope.' He nodded sympathetically.

The tension was creeping up the back of her neck and encircling her head. He hadn't changed. Beneath all the charm, all the affected concern, he was still the same Jeremy.

Aware of both secretaries' soft intake of breath, and their gaze bouncing, like spectators at a tennis match, from herself to Jeremy and back again, she gritted her teeth. 'Let's go into the office, shall we?'

'Yours or mine?'

The apparent innocence of the question did not fool her for an instant. He was marking his territory. But the shock of seeing him again was beginning to wear off and Laura's brain clicked into top gear.

'Well, as you'll be deputising for Dennis until he returns, it's probably best if you use *his* office.' She smiled serenely. 'Lisa, make that coffee for two, please.' And sailed past Jeremy into Dennis's room. He hurried in behind her and went at once to stand behind the desk. *Establishing his position,* Laura thought grimly.

'Laura,' his voice was smooth as butter, 'there is something we had better get straight.' His teeth flashed briefly. 'There's nothing *temporary* about my appointment as project manager. I told you in my letter that I'd applied for it. You can't have forgotten?'

Laura blinked. The letter. She had torn it up, unopened and unread.

'I mean, with my experience, I was the logical choice for the job.' He smirked with self-satisfaction. 'Head Office obviously thought so too. Oh, lord,' his face crumpled in counterfeit dismay, 'you hadn't applied for it, had you? No wonder you weren't keen to come in today. What a disappointment.'

Laura remained silent. She knew there was no point in saying she hadn't applied. Jeremy would believe what he chose to believe and would twist anything she said to suit himself.

He sat down in Dennis's swivel armchair, resting his hands on the leather arms. He did not invite her to sit and Laura knew the omission was deliberate. He was making it clear that she was a subordinate.

Despite all the seething within her, Laura was sharp enough to realise that if he found it necessary to stand on rank, something Dennis had never done, Jeremy must be feeling insecure, even threatened. Could there be something in what Brent had said? Could Jeremy be jealous?

'Naturally, I was terribly sorry to hear of old Dennis's illness. Some people just can't handle pressure. It's very sad, but there it is. Still, it's an ill wind, as they say.' He flashed another of his wide, insincere smiles at her and Laura wondered how she could ever have imagined herself in love with him. He was as phony as a three-dollar bill.

'Anyway, at least it's given us this marvellous opportunity to work together again.' He seemed slightly discomfited by her continued silence. 'And of course, there's ... well ... now you've had a little time to reflect and consider, to think over my proposition, what do you say?'

Laura frowned. What was he talking about? What proposition? *It must have been in the letter.*

She was spared the necessity of replying by Josefa knocking, then putting her head around the door.

'Miss Jefford, Captain Lincoln is on the line for Mr Lewis, shall I take a message or will you speak to him?'

'Will you excuse me?' Laura said politely to Jeremy and turned towards the connecting door with her own office.

'Take it here,' Jeremy said at once, gesturing towards the phone. 'The sooner I learn what's going on around this place, the better.' He smiled, but Laura sensed the threat in his words.

'Thank you, Josefa, put the call through.' As the secretary left, Laura realised that both girls, despite his charm and golden-boy looks, were reserving judgement on Jeremy Grainger.

'Who are these people?' Jeremy asked.

'Sam Lincoln is captain of the port,' Laura replied.

'And what about this Lewis chap? Who is he? One of our employees?'

Despite her tension, Laura could not prevent a smile as she shook her head. 'No. Captain Lincoln wants to speak to Brent Lewis, the shipping journalist.'

A variety of expressions played over Jeremy's face. Predominating were shock and displeasure.

The phone buzzed and Laura picked it up. 'Good morning, Captain. No, he's not, I'm afraid . . . yes, this afternoon . . . of course . . . Mr George Manson of Gibrepair. Yes, I'm sure he'll be delighted. It was most thoughtful of you. Thanks so much.' Jeremy had extended his hand and was making flickering movements with his fingers, silently demanding the phone. 'Would you hold on just a second?' Laura said into the receiver and passed it to Jeremy. 'Excuse me,' she said with icy politeness, and walked briskly through into her own office, closing the connecting door on Jeremy's peremptory, 'Wait——'

Standing at the window, gazing out at the low, black clouds, Laura took several deep breaths. How was she going to *stand* this?

Through the thin walls she could hear Jeremy's voice, full of bluff good cheer and she winced. 'Captain Lincoln, *Sam*, Jeremy Grainger here. I've taken over from Dennis Sanderson. He's ill...yes, most unfortunate...no, we've no idea, I'm afraid, but it will be quite a while. In fact, considering his age it might not be considered advisable for him to return.'

Laura heard the false report and a spurt of anger shook her. Then Jeremy's tone changed.

'No...well, no... Of course I didn't mean...Sam, you misunderstood me——'

She covered her mouth with her fingers as she remembered grizzled, leathery, weather-beaten Sam Lincoln was five years older than Dennis and, by the sound of things, was making it clear to Jeremy that age had nothing to do with ability.

She heard the receiver replaced with a clatter that betrayed ill-concealed temper. She waited for the intercom to buzz and Jeremy to summon her once more. What would she do if he did? Go meekly? Permit *him* to set the tone of their working relationship?

Dennis had treated her as an equal. Jeremy, it seemed, was finding it necessary to drive home his superior position. He could not make it plainer if he jumped on the desk and shouted, 'I'm the boss!' Yet there was no way he could possibly handle all the work alone. He *needed* her.

The same thought must finally have dawned on him for the communicating door opened and, as Laura looked round, she saw him rubbing his hands, his mouth twisted in a smile that was a half-sneer. 'A bit tetchy, isn't he, our port captain?'

'I've never found him so,' Laura said truthfully.

'Well, you wouldn't, being a woman. He'd be all sweetness and light to you.' It sounded like an accusation, and Laura sighed.

Lisa hovered in the doorway of Dennis's office with the tray of coffee. 'I—you weren't—shall I——'

'Thanks, Lisa,' Laura reassured her with a smile, angry and saddened at the change of atmosphere in the office. In place of the easy camaraderie laced with respect, there was unease, even suspicion. 'Just put it on my desk.'

Jeremy waited until the girl had gone, then wagged a roguish finger at Laura. 'You haven't given me an answer.'

Laura's mind raced. Did she allow the conversation to revert to whatever it was he had said in his letter? Should she admit right here and now she didn't know what he was talking about because she hadn't read it? Did she tell him, straight out, that she had torn up the letter because she wanted nothing whatever to do with him and that it didn't matter *what* it said, it was of no conceivable interest to her?

Her feelings about him now were exactly the same as when she had glimpsed his handwriting on the envelope. No, that wasn't true. If anything her aversion was even stronger. But everything else had changed.

She could no longer shut him out of her mind and her life. He was here and she had to work with him. Unless she went back on her commitment to Dennis. Brent had read her correctly. She could not do that. Her initial reaction, her plan to request a transfer, had been born of shock and fear. Jeremy was Acting Managing Director and Project Manager. In those roles he could demand, and receive, her total loyalty. As for the rest, it was naïve to imagine he would not bring up their past relationship at some time. All she could do was try to anticipate and head him off.

'Indeed.' She nodded and began to pour the coffee, proud that her hand was quite steady. 'You were asking about Brent Lewis.'

Though it was obvious he had, briefly, forgotten about the journalist, as Laura passed him the coffee cup she saw a frown mar the golden-brown smoothness of his forehead.

'What exactly is Brent Lewis doing in Gibraltar?'

Laura sat down behind her desk and drew her cup towards her. 'He's writing a series of articles on the expansion and development of the port.' With a polite smile she indicated the chair on the far side of the desk. 'Please do sit down.'

Jeremy arranged the creases in his trousers carefully before crossing one leg over the other. 'Why would Captain Lincoln expect to find him here?'

'Because Dennis thought it a good idea for our company to show him around, introduce him to all the people he needs to talk to, and be generally helpful.'

Jeremy was silent as he digested this. 'Makes sense,' he grudged. 'In fact it's a damn good public relations exercise. Can't say I like the bloke. He's an arrogant bastard.' Laura bit the inside of her lip. 'Still, this is too good an opportunity to miss. It won't do me any harm at all with Head Office.' His brow was deeply furrowed and he seemed to be thinking aloud. 'I don't know how I'm going to fit it in with everything else.' He looked up as an idea struck him, the frown replaced by a brilliant smile. 'But that's the whole point of having a personal assistant, isn't it, to share the office-work.'

Laura didn't believe what she was hearing. 'You mean *you're* going to show him around?'

Jeremy seemed surprised at the question. 'Of course.'

CHAPTER SIX

LAURA still couldn't believe Jeremy was serious. 'But you've only just arrived here. You don't know anyone.'

'Really, Laura,' he did not hide his irritation, 'what has that to do with anything? I can't sit around here waiting for people to come to me. The best and quickest way for me to get to know everyone who matters is by going out and meeting them. Who better to introduce me around than Brent Lewis? Anyone who is anyone in shipping knows him. I couldn't have a more effective calling-card.'

Laura stared at him. She had always known he was ambitious. At the beginning she had admired his drive and determination, especially as he had seemed to understand *her* need to succeed. But she detected an added facet now, a hunger which bordered on desperation.

'But it was supposed to be the other way around. Dennis——'

He cut her short. 'Dennis isn't here now. I am. The Phoenix Group has given the Press every possible assistance in the past. I think we can rely on them, or in this case, on Brent Lewis, to return the favour now. It's as much in his interest as ours. After all, he'd have to talk to all these people anyway, so taking me along will do *him* a bit of good, add a bit of weight, so to speak.'

Laura would have laughed out loud at the very idea of Brent needing anyone, much less Jeremy, to *add*

98

weight to his meetings and interviews, were it not so horribly clear that Jeremy was deadly serious.

'In fact...' he mused, voicing the idea as it occurred to him '... I think I'll get him to do a publicity release for the local press and the international shipping papers, about my promotion and transfer from Rotterdam.'

'Jeremy,' Laura was becoming concerned, 'I don't think you understand——'

'No,' he held up his hand and smiled, 'it's you who don't understand. Your relationship with Dennis is none of my business. Though when you broke off our engagement, I couldn't help but wonder——'

Laura jumped to her feet sending her chair spinning backwards. 'Now just a minute.' She made an enormous effort to keep her voice quiet and even. 'My relationship with Dennis has never been anything but strictly professional. If you know him as well as you *say* you do, you should know he's a devoted family man. And as for ending our engagement, it had nothing to do with anyone else. The decision was entirely mine.' She wanted to add that it was the wisest move she had ever made and she had not regretted it for one single instant, but the realisation that, for the time being, for Dennis's sake, she had to stay and work with this man, made her hold back.

'OK, OK,' he soothed, 'perhaps I was a bit out of order there.'

'You certainly were.' Laura was not going to be placated easily.

'These things do happen. You are a very attractive woman.' His smile widened. 'Working with you every day, there'd have to be something wrong with a man for his thoughts not to stray occasionally.'

His flattery left her unmoved. '*If* Dennis's did, which I very much doubt, he had the common sense, and the consideration, to keep them to himself.'

'Oh, lord, I really have put my foot in it.' The boyish charm was in full flood and his expression was chastened and regretful. 'It isn't easy for me, seeing you again, working together, especially after the way we parted.'

'It's not easy for me either,' Laura said with complete honesty.

Jeremy's face brightened at once and he stood up. 'Perhaps I came on a bit strong. But, to tell you the truth, I was nervous.' He shrugged. 'Ridiculous, isn't it? I mean, we're both adults.' He fingered his cuff-links. They were large and gold and had his initials inscribed on them in ornate script. 'I've kept myself informed of your progress and I must admit, it's been quite impressive.'

Was it her imagination, or did she detect a sour note?

'Anyway, we both have the good of the company at heart, and the same aim, to bring this project to a successful conclusion. That's right, isn't it?' He searched her face.

Laura nodded slowly. She could not argue with what he was saying, yet something jarred.

'I'm glad we understand one another. We must both make a real effort to overcome our feelings about the past.' His gaze fell away. 'I'm not afraid to admit I was deeply hurt. I think it was your ingratitude that wounded me most. But,' he forestalled any interruption, 'I accept you must have had your reasons.' His tone made it clear that whatever they were, they were totally inadequate and no excuse at all for what he had suffered.

Laura's fingers curled into her palms.

'What matters now is the future,' he went on, 'the future of the project and the company. I'm not exaggerating when I say they lie in our hands, Laura. A change of leadership in mid-stream, so to speak, does not exactly build confidence in City financial circles. I know, I know,' he said as she opened her mouth, 'Dennis couldn't help being ill.'

To Laura it sounded like an accusation of carelessness and incompetence.

'But now it's up to us to present a united front and show that it's business *even better* than usual.' He leaned towards her. 'We must help each other as much as possible. My way of doing things is likely to be different from Dennis's. You may even find that *your* role changes. Just remember that the *objective* is the same. And remember the good times we shared, Laura. There were quite a few, you know.' He straightened up. 'Now, Dennis handled all the finances, I believe?' His brisk change of mood took her by surprise.

'Oh—er—yes.'

'Then the first thing I'd better do is examine the books. Shall we go through to my office?' Flashing her a brilliant smile he walked out, leaving her to follow.

'No,' Brent said evenly.

Jeremy managed to keep his smile in place, but Laura could see it was an effort. They were in her office. Brent had just arrived and Jeremy, hearing Brent's voice, had marched in to join them.

'Why not? It seems a perfectly reasonable suggestion.'

Brent looked at him once more, his expression cold. 'It wasn't a suggestion, it was a statement of intent. I'm surprised you thought I would even consider it.' He turned to Laura. 'Are you ready?'

'Where are you going?' Jeremy butted in before Laura could speak.

'To lunch first, and then we have a business appointment in town.'

'So what's wrong with taking me with you?'

Brent faced him once more. 'Is that a serious question?'

'I never joke about my work.'

'Nor do I,' Brent said, 'and the idea is ludicrous.'

Laura swallowed hard as Jeremy's battle to contain his anger showed in the working of his face. Did Brent have to be quite so scathing?

'I'm sorry you feel that way,' Jeremy said stiffly, then a look of cunning flitted briefly across his features. 'Perhaps you don't appreciate the pressures of my position.'

'I'm sure you're right.' Brent was cool. 'Now if you'll excuse us——'

'You see, I don't think I'm going to be able to spare Laura from the office,' Jeremy said, deeply regretful.

'I'm sorry to hear that.' Brent didn't sound sorry, Laura thought. In fact it was virtually impossible to guess what his real feelings were. From the moment Jeremy had joined them in the office, the atmosphere had been electric. With politeness barely concealing their mutual dislike, the two men had metaphorically circled one another like wolves, the rogue challenging the leader's supremacy. But though she and Jeremy both worked for Phoenix and Brent was the outsider, it was *Jeremy* and not Brent whom she saw as the troublemaker and from whom she sensed the greatest threat.

Brent went on, 'I imagined, foolishly it appears, that my arrangement with Dennis Sanderson would be honoured.'

'What exactly was that arrangement?'

'That Laura—Miss Jefford—as a gesture of courtesy on the company's behalf, would introduce me to various people connected with Gibraltar's development as a port.'

'Wait,' Jeremy's smugness was shattered, 'are you saying *Laura* has been acting as your guide and——'

'Yes,' Brent replied.

'Is this true?' Jeremy demanded, swinging round, his forehead puckered into a glowering frown. She did not have time to answer.

'Grainger,' Brent's voice was as smooth and cold as ice, 'are you calling me a liar?'

Swivelling back to Brent, Jeremy recognised his gaffe and made desperate attempts to cover it. 'No.' He shook his head quickly. Regaining control, he smiled, but it was no more than a contraction of his facial muscles. 'Of course not. I was surprised, that was all.'

'By what?' Laura asked.

'First of all that you hadn't bothered to tell me, and second, that Dennis didn't handle that side of things himself.'

'I would have told you, if you'd given me the chance,' she replied calmly. 'Anyway, I didn't do all of it. Dennis and I shared it between us. It worked very well.'

'I bet,' Jeremy muttered tightly. Making an effort to combat what was eating at him he turned to Brent. 'Well, it looks like you and Laura have been having a high old time.'

'I wouldn't say that,' Laura countered, her voice quietly firm.

'But you've obviously been out a lot together.'

'As much as necessary.' Brent's eyes were narrowed. 'In fact, as I have already mentioned, we have an appointment this afternoon.' He turned to Laura. 'We ought to——'

'May I ask with whom?' Jeremy interrupted, his face a smiling mask. But Laura could see fury glittering in his eyes and unease lay, cold and solid, in her stomach.

'A director of the Chamber of Commerce. I gather Dennis did not find him particularly easy to get on with. But Laura, with her tact and diplomacy, had no difficulties at all.' Brent glanced at her, one corner of his mouth lifting.

Unable to resist, she grinned back, recalling how little of either she had been able to use when the obnoxious little man had left her with no choice but to put him firmly in his place.

Jeremy caught the exchange and a spasm of jealous rage contorted his face. Seeing it, Laura's unease grew.

'I really don't know,' Jeremy shook his head slowly. 'I need Laura here, you see.' There was a silence, then Brent stuck his hands in his trouser pockets and rocked gently backwards and forwards on his heels.

'Of course, I can't *force* you to allow Laura to continue helping me, though she has undoubtedly made my job very much easier, which in turn has reflected well on the company.' He paused to let the full significance of his words sink in. 'But if you really *need* her here,' he shrugged, 'there's nothing more to be said. I was given to understand the project was running with enviable smoothness. It seems I must be mistaken.'

Jeremy's head jerked up and Laura held her breath.

'Why should you imagine that you are mistaken?' Jeremy demanded.

'Surely it's obvious?'

'No.' Jeremy shook his head. 'You'd better explain.'

'Dennis, as Managing Director of Phoenix Developments, assigned his Girl Friday to me, an internationally famous journalist working on articles of great importance to every company involved in Gibraltar's expansion.' He spoke without pride or false modesty, simply stating the facts. 'Now you have decided to withdraw that assistance. If your decision is based on purely personal motives, it's hardly wise.' He shook his head. 'Reneging on a goodwill gesture to the Press?' Brent made tutting noises. 'What ever happened to public relations? The only other possible reason I can think of is that Phoenix has something to hide and you don't have Dennis's faith in Laura's ability to keep a secret.' His words fell like pebbles into a glassy pool and, in the silence, the ripples spread ever wider. Brent glanced at Laura. 'I wonder which it could be,' he said softly.

She fought to keep her face expressionless, but her heart fluttered like a trapped bird. *He can't possibly know. It's just a stab in the dark,* she repeated over and over again.

'What the hell are you talking about?' Jeremy's astonishment, with its undertone of anger, was utterly convincing.

Laura knew she *ought* to have told him. Keeping the financial crisis facing the company to herself was quite wrong. As Dennis's replacement, he was entitled to know. But Dennis had said the whole matter would be sorted out within a day or two. If Jeremy had arrived, as everyone had expected, a few days later, it would all have been settled. She was sure to hear this afternoon, tomorrow at the very latest. With Jeremy taking every opportunity to belittle Dennis's achievements, and by implication hers too, she had acted on an impulse, spurred on by anger and resentment, and said simply that their accounts were all in order and that they had funds to meet all payments. *The bank would sanction the extra money.* It had to. Jeremy had not pressed to see the statements and with very little effort she had diverted his attention to the plans and the surveyor's and driller's reports.

'Of course Phoenix has nothing to hide.' This was Jeremy at his most assertive, totally secure in the knowledge that he was right.

Brent looked puzzled and, for an instant, uncertain. Laura felt almost sick with relief.

'My decision to keep Laura in the office is based purely on the need to have her acquaint me with the way things have been run. Hardly the sinister motive you are implying. But then,' his smile was very nearly a sneer, 'I suppose that's one of the problems of being a reporter. If there isn't any news you have to manufacture it.'

Brent did not react to the taunt. 'It's still rather a waste of time, isn't it?' he observed. 'As, doubtless, you will wish to change everything.'

Don't antagonise him, Laura wanted to plead with Brent. *Don't make things worse than they already are.*

'If you want to learn your way around the office, I would suggest that Dennis's secretary would be of far more use to you,' Brent stated mildly. 'It seems extremely wasteful of Laura's talents to confine her to such trivial matters when everyone I've spoken to is so admiring of her abilities as the company's trouble-shooter.'

'I hardly think you are in a position to tell me how to do my job,' Jeremy hissed, the veneer of charm wearing dangerously thin.

'Oh, I don't know,' Brent mused. 'Sometimes the outsider sees more of the game.'

The more wound up Jeremy became, the more Brent seemed to relax. But Laura knew he was not missing the slightest change in expression or stance. Brent Lewis read body language like other people read the printed word. It was just one of the things that made him so dangerous. She had to put a stop to this before it all got out of hand.

'Jeremy,' she stood up, 'could we have a word in private?' She started towards Dennis's office, glancing at Brent over her shoulder. 'Would you excuse us for a moment?'

Silently, he gestured for them to go ahead and as Jeremy followed her, tight-lipped and pale with barely contained anger, Brent strolled to the window and looked out.

'So,' Jeremy's mouth was twisted as he turned on her the instant she closed the door, 'you've been——'

'Listen,' Laura interrupted urgently, before he could launch into the tirade, '*we both have the good of the company at heart,* isn't that what you said? We both want to bring this project to a successful conclusion. Those were *your* words, Jeremy, less than two hours ago. Have you changed your mind?'

She could see he was taken aback by her directness. 'Of course not,' he began testily, 'but——'

'No *buts*, Jeremy,' she cut in. 'Working with Brent Lewis was not my idea. I didn't want the assignment.' Curiosity sparked in his eyes and she hurried on before he could interrupt. 'I tried more than once to get out of it. I wasn't successful. You can pull me out. You have the power. But if you do, you'll be making a powerful enemy. Brent Lewis is not a man to cross. How would it reflect on the company?' She waited a moment, then added, 'And on you?'

The same thought had obviously occurred to Jeremy. Already he was calmer, more in command of himself. He fingered the heavy cuff-links, frowning. Laura could almost see options being considered and discarded.

'Perhaps I was a trifle hasty. The man has an unfortunate habit of rubbing me the wrong way. I find him arrogant, condescending and a real pain in the—never mind. I think, on reflection it would be best if we let things stand. Go with Lewis, do whatever he expects in the way of introductions and so on. But *I* expect to be kept fully informed.'

Laura was tempted to snap a salute and reply 'Yessir,' but it was only fleeting. Jeremy's sense of humour was almost non-existent and irony was lost on him. He would probably take her seriously.

He gave her a lofty smile. 'You can brief me over dinner tonight. I'm told my hotel has one of the best restaurants on the Rock.'

'I'm afraid that won't be possible,' Laura said at once.

'Oh?' His smile faded. 'Got another date?'

'I shall be working.'

'You still have to eat,' he pointed out. 'Besides, there are a lot of things we still have to discuss.' The business-like briskness was replaced by a wheedling note. 'Come on, Laura, for old times' sake?'

Laura cupped her elbows, pressing her arms against her stomach, feeling tension mounting within her. This was the moment of truth. If she didn't face up to it now and make her position absolutely clear to Jeremy, the situation would keep on recurring, and grow ever more complicated.

Her throat was uncomfortably dry. 'Th-there are no old times I wish to remember, Jeremy. What's past is past, finished.'

He stared at her, then laughed. 'You don't mean that. We were a team, you and I, a really great team. We could be again. Call it Fate, call it what you like, but it was meant to be.' He took a step forward, stopping as she turned away. 'You've proved you can make it on your own. I always knew you could.' It took a tremendous effort of will for Laura not to laugh in his face. 'But together there'd be no stopping us, Laura. This is our second chance, a fresh start.' His voice vibrated with warmth and persuasion. It was almost convincing. But Laura had seen the other side of him, the viciousness and spite. She remembered the evening they parted, when all his pent-up frustration and jealousy had erupted like pus from an abscess, and he had tried, verbally, to destroy her.

No mistake had been too small, no error too petty for him to recall and hurl at her. No detail of her slender physique had escaped his lacerating criticism, and no personal doubt or worry confided in a moment of trust and tenderness remained sacred. He had stopped at nothing in his attempt to break her spirit and totally annihilate what was left of her belief in herself.

Even now, after all this time, the memory of that evening made her feel sick and shaky. But it also strengthened her resolve. She might have to work with him, *but that was all*.

She forced herself to look at him straight in the eye. 'I'm sorry, Jeremy.' And for the moment she was. Sorry for him, for the darkness that surrounded him. Sorry that he had learned nothing. But it didn't last.

She could see from his expression he still did not accept she meant it. She could hardly credit his egotism. Could he honestly believe that after what he had done she would simply agree to forgive and forget? But he did. In fact, recalling what he had said earlier about her ingratitude hurting him, he appeared to think that he should be doing the forgiving.

Laura felt slow, deep anger begin to burn within her. She tried to extinguish it, to block it out. What had happened was in the past. It was over. *It could not hurt or touch her now.* The anger faded, but her determination was even stronger. 'I'm sorry,' she repeated.

She watched him change as realisation dawned. The vibrancy flickered out like a blown candle. His mouth

thinned and the petulant droop grew more pronounced.
He raised a hand and with a flattened palm smoothed
the golden hair at his temple.

'You're making a grave mistake, Laura.' The note of
threat, the hint of warning, were unmistakable.

There were many retorts she could have made, and
the urge to retaliate was so strong she had to fasten the
inside of her lip with her teeth to contain it.

Tasting blood, she turned away and went to the door.
Grasping the handle, she spoke carefully, keeping her
face and voice devoid of expression. 'I shall probably
come back to the office between four and five to finish
the correspondence and deal with anything else that has
cropped up. If you wish, I can give you a verbal report
then.'

'I may be out,' he snapped, throwing himself into
Dennis's swivel chair. 'If so, I expect a written account
of the meeting, plus a list of everyone you have introduced Lewis to so far, and those he still wishes to meet.'

'Wouldn't it be simpler to ask him yourself?' she
suggested, realising as the words left her mouth they
would have been better unsaid.

'Those are my instructions,' he replied crisply. 'As my
assistant, it's your job to see that they are carried out.
There will be no argument and no discussion. Is that
understood?'

'Perfectly,' Laura replied. She was going to pay for
turning him down. That much was clear. What she did
not yet know was just how high the price would be.

As she emerged, Brent turned from the window and
looked closely at her, a frown forming. 'Are you all
right?'

She nodded, forcing a grin. 'Of course. Why shouldn't
I be?'

His face darkened. 'There's blood on your teeth.'

In two strides Brent had reached her. He seized her arms, making her jump. His anger was fearsome. 'Did he...?' He set her aside and lunged forward to the door.

'No!' Laura cried, grabbing his coat to stop him. He looked down at her, his eyes as hard and black as coal. 'I bit my lip, that was all.' She could see his doubt. He was visibly fighting the urge to confront Jeremy. His fists were clenched, the knuckles gleaming white. 'If he laid a finger on you——'

Laura was terrified. 'He didn't, honestly!' She had to convince him. 'Physical violence never was Jeremy's style.' Cuts and bruises healed far more quickly than the wounds a warped mind like his could inflict.

'I'm perfectly all right, really.' She shrugged, trying to make light of it, and dabbed at her lip again. Her blood was jewel-bright on the white tissue. 'I'll have to find some other way of controlling my feelings. My tongue is suffering from battle fatigue.'

Brent seized her shoulders. 'You're sure you're OK?' She nodded. 'Then let's get out of here.' She could feel the tension emanating from him. 'I need some fresh air.'

'I don't suppose I helped, did I?' he said as they crossed the foyer to the main doors.

'Not much,' she agreed.

'I'm sorry.'

They were silent as they walked along the street, then oblivious of the surprise and curiosity of the passers-by, Brent caught her arm and pulled her roughly towards him, his fingers biting into her flesh. 'But I'm not letting you go, Laura.' He cupped her face with one hand. 'You're far too valuable to me.'

She caught her breath and her heart gave a mighty leap. 'Oh, Brent,' she murmured, her eyes shining.

He grinned down at her. 'Let golden-boy find out for himself where the typewriter ribbons are kept.' He dropped a kiss on her forehead and tucking her arm through his, started talking about a restaurant he had seen where they could have lunch before going on to their appointment.

Laura tried hard to match his mood, but the sun had lost its warmth, and the light had gone out of the day.

Was that all that mattered to him? That he had won the confrontation? Got his own way? Forced Jeremy to concede defeat and abide by the arrangement? Was she nothing more than a pawn with each of them fighting for possession?

An indefinable sadness weighed heavily on her. The restaurant was crowded and lively, the food delicious. But she wasn't hungry.

Determined to put up a good show, she talked and laughed, certain Brent had not noticed how little she had, in fact, eaten.

The interview was a great success. Puffed up like a pigeon, full of self-importance, the director expounded his views concerning the Rock's economy at great length, talking exclusively to Brent. Laura was content to watch and listen. She realised the little man had to assert himself to regain his pride. His loss of face had not been her choice, he had brought it on himself. *Which brought her back to Jeremy.*

When they were once more out on the street, she remembered the message Sam Lincoln had left for Brent. He wanted her to go with him to the ship-repair yard, but pleading pressure of work, without mentioning the extra Jeremy had demanded, she returned to the office.

As she walked in, Josefa looked round from the telex machine. 'There was a call from London. Mr Bradley of Bradley & Harding.'

Laura froze. *The bank.* 'When?'

'About half an hour ago. I told Mr Bradley I had a number for you and phoned straight away, but they said you'd already gone. I——'

'That's all right, Josefa,' Laura broke in. 'Could you call him back, at once, please. Is Mr Grainger in?'

Josefa shook her head. 'He went out soon after you and Mr Lewis left. He said he was going down to see Captain Lincoln and then to pay a courtesy call on the chairman of Callero's.'

Laura hesitated, but only for an instant. Clearly, Jeremy was losing no time in establishing himself among the shipping-business fraternity. Callero's was the largest group of companies in Gibraltar, with interests in repair, bunkering, and towage, as well as acting as ship agents and freight forwarders. She had met Luke Callero several times. With graceful manners and old-world charm he had masked his surprise as Dennis introduced her, and on subsequent meetings and telephone conversations had been most helpful.

At this moment, however, she did not really care where Jeremy was. She was just relieved that he was out, and she could make the call without fear of interruption.

Sitting forward on the edge of her chair, she had just taken several deep breaths in an unsuccessful attempt to combat her nervousness, when Josefa buzzed.

'I have Mr Bradley on the line.'

Laura picked up the receiver and moistened her lips. 'Good afternoon, Mr Bradley. I'm so sorry I wasn't here to receive your earlier call. Had I known...' They exchanged brief pleasantries about the weather, comparing rainfall for April in London and Gibraltar, while Laura's stomach clenched and unclenched and her nerves were stretched ever tighter. She kept her voice light and relaxed. But her mind was racing.

Why didn't he just say it? Yes or no. Was he trying
to soften his refusal? Why would he bother? Because it
was good business practice to stay on friendly terms with
clients. Once they were successful they might want to
expand. They would need further funding. *As soon as
you've proved you can make it without our money, we'll
lend you all you need.*

In a rare moment of cynicism Laura decided that banks
were organisations that pressed an umbrella upon you
when the sun was shining, only to snatch it away again
at the first drop of rain.

'...I'm sure you can see our point,' Mr Bradley's
mellifluous tones echoed in her ear. With a start, Laura
realised she had missed something. But there didn't seem
to be much doubt about his decision. He was just sugar-
ing the pill.

She swallowed hard. 'Yes.' She stared blindly at the
wall. 'Yes, I quite understand.'

That was it then. All that Dennis had worked so hard
for, all her own efforts, wiped out. Jeremy would have
to be told. He would have to suspend all work on the
project and inform the contractors. God knew how many
men would be put out of work. The company could be
sued for breaking contracts. In the meantime she and
Jeremy would have to make frantic efforts to secure
finance from other sources. That alone would be far
from easy, and Jeremy's reaction simply did not bear
thinking about.

The phone was slippery in her hand and she switched
it to her other ear, flexing fingers stiff and aching from
the strain.

'...Mr Sanderson's wholehearted recommendation
of yourself, plus his own considerable experience in this
field. So after careful consideration——' Laura crossed
her fingers and closed her eyes. She held her breath and

waited, hardly daring to hope '—the Board has agreed to the terms Mr Sanderson put forward. The money will be credited to the Phoenix account by 10 a.m. tomorrow morning. A letter of confirmation is in the post.'

Laura leaned back in her chair, limp with relief, and covering the mouthpiece with her hand, let her breath out with a rush. 'Thank you, Mr Bradley,' she said calmly, as though there had never been a moment's doubt. 'Yes, I'll tell him. Many thanks. Goodbye.'

She replaced the receiver and stretched her arms above her head, ridding herself of all the accumulated tension. *They had won.* The project was safe. She let her hands flop over the arms of the chair and tried to relax completely. But something niggled. Something Mr Bradley had said.

She sat up. It wasn't what he *had* said, it was what he *hadn't*.

He had not asked after Dennis, or mentioned Jeremy. *They didn't know Dennis was ill or that Jeremy had replaced him.*

Laura thought hard. Dennis had collapsed *after* the meeting. He couldn't have known it was going to happen. The bank had accepted Dennis's proposals. The fact that someone else would be putting them into operation was surely irrelevant.

Her doubts evaporated and happiness lifted her spirits. A smile danced at the corners of her mouth as she leaned forward to press the intercom switch. Margaret would be spending most of her time at the hospital, so it would be almost impossible to reach her by phone. Phoning the hospital direct was not a good idea either, as there was no guarantee the message would reach Dennis. 'Lisa, send a cable to Mr Sanderson, care of his home address. The message is "Bank confirmed project assured. Get well soon. Laura". Have you got that?'

'Yes.' Lisa read the message back. 'You want it sent immediately?'

'Please. Then come in and we'll clear this backlog.'

The next hour flew. Laura glanced at her watch and was amazed to see it was almost five. 'OK, that's the lot for today.'

Lisa rose, closing her notebook, and picking up the bundle of files. 'Are you staying on?'

Laura nodded. She still had the report to do for Jeremy. Though with luck it wouldn't take long.

'Shall I make you some tea before I go?'

'You're a gem.' Laura smiled her thanks.

Lisa sighed, 'I know,' and flashed a cheeky grin as she disappeared.

Laura opened her pen and pulled a large, lined pad towards her. The intercom buzzed.

'Shall I bring two cups?' Lisa enquired. 'Mr Lewis has just arrived.'

Laura's heart soared. Brent. She could face him now. There was no more need for secrecy and subterfuge. 'Yes please, and ask him to——'

The door opened and in he walked.

'Never mind, Lisa.' She released the switch and stood up. 'You might at least wait until——'

'I'm summoned?'

'Invited,' she corrected. 'How was your meeting with George Manson?'

'Very useful.' He perched on the corner of her desk. 'You should have come. You'd have found it extremely interesting. Unless you've already heard about their plans.'

Laura shook her head. 'No, I haven't, but the invitation was for you alone. In any case, I couldn't have spared the time this afternoon.'

'Been busy?'

She nodded and tried to suppress her smile.

Brent's gaze was quizzical. 'Grainger must be out.'

She looked up. 'Yes. How did you know?'

'He'd have been in here by now. Besides, you are looking much happier than you were earlier.'

Laura made a brief gesture, brushing the mention of Jeremy aside. Picking up the folders she no longer needed, she crossed to the filing-cabinet. 'It's got nothing to do with him.'

'I see. Some good news then?'

'You could say that.' She pulled open the top drawer. 'The money came through.'

For an instant she was absolutely still. Then, holding the front edge of the drawer, she turned her head. 'I beg your pardon?' *She must have misheard. He couldn't have said . . .*

'The money came through. From your backers. Extra funds for the project.' He spoke with the calm authority of someone who was quite certain of his facts.

Laura stared at him. 'You *knew*?'

CHAPTER SEVEN

HE nodded slowly. 'Yes, I knew.'

'But *how*? How did you find out? Who told you?' Realising she sounded as though it was something to feel guilty about and ashamed of, some of Laura's shock turned to anger and spilled over. 'All this time you've——'

He raised both hands to silence her. 'If you want answers, you'll have to stop firing questions at me.'

She slammed the drawer shut and slapped the rest of the folders down on top of the cabinet. 'All right. Explain. But it had better be good, because——' She stopped abruptly as the door opened and Lisa came in with the tea.

Oblivious of the tense atmosphere, the secretary flashed Brent a smile which combined yearning with the realisation that she was wasting her time. As Laura silently seethed, half relieved, half furious at the interruption, Brent winked at Lisa. Dropping the tray on to the desk with a clatter, Lisa blushed a bright pink, dimpled prettily, and scuttled out.

'Well?' Laura demanded as soon as the door had closed. 'What about some of these answers? How long have you known?' But much of her anger had gone, leaving chagrin and a growing sense of hurt in its place.

Brent caught her hands. Reluctant, uncertain, she allowed him to draw her forward. He sat on the edge of her desk and intuitively she understood it had been a calculated move, to reduce his height, to set his eye-level

118

lower than hers and diminish her feeling of being
threatened. Raising her left hand to his mouth, he kissed
the back of it. His lips were warm and soft, and the
thrill of their touch shivered through her, melting the
last of her anger. 'I had heard the rumour before I came
here.'

'But you were in Canada,' she blurted.

'They do have telephones, *and* Telex, *and* Fax ma-
chines. They're really quite civilised,' he mocked gently.

Laura flushed. 'That wasn't—I didn't——'

'I know what you meant,' he cut in. 'There aren't
many of us in shipping, Laura. We all know one another.
If one of us gets a tip-off or hears something which isn't
relevant to the story he's working on, it's usually passed
on to a colleague who *is* in a position to use it. Which
is what happened in this case.' His expression hardened,
became cynical. 'In business, the bad news always travels
fastest.'

'And you're not going to tell me who told you,' she
stated, already knowing the answer, but needing
confirmation.

He shook his head. 'It wouldn't help if I did, because
the person who told me got it from somebody else. Besides, it's an unbreakable rule. No journalist ever re-
veals his sources. Some of my colleagues have been
imprisoned for contempt of court for refusing to name
an informant. I've had a couple of near misses myself. You see, there has to be trust, and it's a very
special——'

'*Trust?*' Laura's laugh was short and harsh. 'I remember you asking me in the caves to trust you.'

'Yes. And you wouldn't.'

'I *couldn't*,' Laura cried. 'It seems a very one-sided
bargain, this *trust* of yours. You expected me to reveal
information which could have destroyed confidence in

the company, yet you're not prepared to tell me how *you* found out about it.' She tried to pull away, but he held her fast.

'One thing I can tell you,' his gaze was clear and direct, his eyes so dark they were almost black, 'the leak did not come from here. Both you and Dennis put up a magnificent front. You particularly.'

Laura didn't know how to react. Was he saying she was a good liar? Was that praise? To be pleased about? Perhaps in this context it was. So much business was conducted on the basis of bluff and counter-bluff, and each day it seemed more lies were necessary. Ethics and ideals were all too easily suffocated by economic expediency. She felt a pang. Was it really something to be proud of? Much as she enjoyed the actual work, was she really *suited* to this job? Certain aspects of it were forcing her to do a lot of heart-searching.

Despite her resolve, she could not hide the hurt that went deeper than all the other emotions his disclosure had provoked. 'Why didn't you tell me you knew? Was it more fun playing cat and mouse with me? Did you get a kick out of watching me make a fool of myself?'

'Is that how it seemed to you?'

She nodded tightly.

'It shouldn't have. You have never looked foolish to me. Laura, I tried to make it clear that you had nothing to fear from me. I thought I'd made my position plain. Unless and until the decision had gone against you and the bank had pulled out, I, *as a journalist*, was not concerned.' He paused, and his voice softened. 'On the other hand, as a friend——'

'A friend?' Laura cried before she could stop herself.

'Yes,' he responded immediately. 'I wanted to *help*. I could see what you were going through. I knew the battle you were having with yourself.'

You don't know the half of it, she thought wildly. 'But how *could* I have told you?' she burst out. 'You're a *journalist*, for heaven's sake. How could I expect you to ignore such a story? One of the companies involved in a massive programme of port development facing financial problems that could close it down? OK, so *you* might not have used it, but if one whisper had leaked to the local paper or the national dailies back home, they'd have made mincemeat of Phoenix. Besides,' she said wearily, her voice dropping, 'I had given Dennis my word.'

'And you don't break promises, do you, Laura?' His gaze was dark, mesmeric. 'Even Grainger doesn't know, does he?'

His statement didn't really surprise her. She was beginning to take his astuteness for granted. Closing her eyes briefly, she shook her head. 'Are you going to tell him?'

He smiled. 'Why should I? What is there to tell—now?'

She made no attempt to hide her relief. 'I know I should have. He had every right to be fully informed, but...'

'But what?' Brent prompted.

'He'd have used it against—against Dennis and all the hard work he's put in, and Dennis isn't here to defend himself.'

'Why should Grainger do that?' Brent asked with deceptive mildness. 'Surely you're all on the same side?'

Laura shook her head. 'Jeremy has made it pretty clear that he wants Dennis's job. If he can cast a shadow over Dennis's name with Head Office, he'll do it.'

Brent's brows formed a thick black bar as he frowned. 'And what about you?'

'What about me?'

His frown deepened. 'Don't play games with me, Laura. He was engaged to you once. You broke it off, and now he has been made your boss. Don't expect me to believe he hasn't brought up the past. A man like Grainger wouldn't be able to resist it.'

Laura chewed her lip, then, reluctantly, nodded.

'I suppose he wanted to pick up the threads again?'

Laura nodded once more.

'What did you say?' Brent's voice had an edge to it. 'And don't tell me it's none of my business.'

The ever-present current arced between them. Her colour high, she held his gaze, answering with total honesty. 'I told him there was nothing I wanted to discuss, no *old times* I wanted to remember. What's past is over, finished.' She swallowed.

Briefly, Brent's features reflected his satisfaction, then his frown returned. 'How did he take it?'

'Not very well,' Laura admitted. She tried to grin. 'I don't think the atmosphere around here is going to be exactly sweetness and light for the next few weeks.'

'What about your job? How will that be affected?'

'I'm not sure, yet. For the moment, I gather everything is to stay the same. I'm to accompany you as arranged——' his fingers tightened on hers and she felt her cheeks grow warm '—but he wants written reports of the meetings we attend, plus a list of the people I introduce you to.' She stopped. 'I really shouldn't be telling you all this.'

'Why not?' he demanded softly. 'It concerns me, doesn't it?'

'Y—e—s,' she allowed, 'but it seems all wrong—disloyal—'

'To whom?' His expression mellowed. 'Oh, Laura,' he murmured, 'do you still not trust me?'

'It's not—yes, yes, I do,' she was hesitant, stumbling over the words as she tried to find the right ones '—it's just that——'

'You've only known me for a few days?' he supplied. *Was that really all it was?* 'It seems——' *a lifetime,* her heart whispered '—a lot longer,' she finished lamely, her eyes dipping away from his.

'Doesn't it just.' She could hear the undercurrent of laughter, saw it gleam in his eyes as he tilted her chin, forcing her to look at him. 'From the moment I walked into Dennis Sanderson's office...' He broke off, his tone changing, becoming steely, almost accusing. 'You were so cool, so self-possessed.'

'You were an arrogant, chauvinist pig,' Laura retorted, flushing as his eyes narrowed dangerously. But his grasp on her hands never slackened.

'Is that all? Nothing more? What about *patronising*? You left that out.'

'On purpose,' she replied, more calmly. 'That was one thing you didn't do. You never talked down to me. But I stand by the rest.'

He lifted her hand and gently bit her knuckles. 'Self-protection,' he admitted.

Laura blinked. *'What?'*

He looked at her hand for a long moment. When at last he did speak he was uncharacteristically hesitant. 'I wasn't ready...I hadn't expected ... Dammit, Laura,' he grated glaring at her, 'there was enough voltage between us to power the National Grid.'

Stunned, Laura stared at him. She *hadn't* imagined it. He had sensed it too. *Right from the first moment.* 'But—but—I thought——' She lapsed into silence, too confused, too overwhelmed, for words.

His eyes narrowed, glittering, as he drew her closer, resting his hands on her hips, his long legs stretched out on either side of her. 'What did you think?'

She shrugged helplessly. 'You seemed so...angry... with me and I didn't know why.'

'How could you? I didn't know myself. Oh there were other things. I was tired. I've done three foreign trips already this year. I shouldn't have taken this job at all really. I needed a rest. But I did come. The last thing I expected was...you.' His hungry gaze searched her face.

'But that evening on the beach...' she faltered.

'It was a marvellous evening, wasn't it?' The hard planes of his face relaxed.

'It started out that way,' she agreed, her lips curving at the memory of their dance on the sand at the water's edge. 'But then...' She broke off. 'You changed. It was so sudden.' She shook her head, unable to go on.

His grip tightened. 'I was fighting the effect you were having on me,' he said quietly. 'I didn't want any emotional entanglements.' His gaze moved over her mouth, down her neck to the hollow of her throat at the opening of her dress. Bowing his head, he rested his forehead gently against her breasts.

Laura caught her breath. What now? Did he still feel that way? She had endured enough pain and treachery with Jeremy to last a lifetime. She couldn't face any more. But Brent had kindled fire where Jeremy had left her untouched and unmoved. He had just admitted to being as deeply affected as she was. At most they had three weeks before he left for Hong Kong. Was she going to deny what she felt because of that?

She hesitated a moment longer then slowly, almost reluctantly brought her hands up and ran them through the springy black hair, smoothing it, feeling the warmth of his scalp, closing her eyes as she inhaled his musky scent. She could hardly believe she was holding him. It was a dream, she never wanted to wake up.

His arms slid around her waist and he pressed her body to his, turning his head to one side.

She gazed down at the hard profile and surprisingly thick dark lashes. As she stroked his face, learning him with her fingertips, the abrasive roughness along his jaw made her smile. Dreams didn't have five-o'clock stubble. This was a very real man.

Brent made a muffled sound and stood up. Laura's hands fell to his shoulders. As she looked into his eyes and saw the fierce hunger, like a sun bursting deep inside her, a million tiny flames seared every nerve. At her quick intake of breath his eyes narrowed and he brought his head down.

With a tenderness that was almost torture he brushed her lips with his own, quick light kisses that teased and tormented until, driven beyond shyness, beyond endurance, she clasped his head, burying her fingers in his hair as her mouth clung to his.

With a deep-throated groan, Brent tightened his arms around her. His tongue, hot and sweet, probed the softness of her mouth, piercing her with shocks like summer lightning.

Laura had never before experienced the powerful sensations that racked her now. Her heart was racing and crushed against Brent's chest, her breasts hurt. But it was an exciting pain and she welcomed it. A dark, rushing whirlwind filled her head and liquid heat poured through her veins.

Brent tore his mouth from hers, his breathing harsh and ragged. He pressed burning kisses to her eyes, temple, ear and throat making her gasp as delicious shudders rippled through her. 'Brent...don't...I...'

'Hush,' he stifled her protests with his lips, then, clasping her to him once more, lifted her off her feet and whirled her round. 'Laura Jefford,' he muttered hoarsely, 'you should be stamped with a Government Health Warning.' He set her down gently.

She quivered inside. Her cheeks were on fire and her mouth, as she raised tentative fingers to her lips, felt different, warm and soft, and slightly swollen.

'Come on, let's go back to the hotel,' he murmured, gently massaging the back of her neck. 'We can bathe and change and I'll take you out to dinner,' he brought his head down, 'eventually,' he whispered and kissed the place where his fingers had been.

Laura leaned against him, her eyes closed, and waited for the room to stop spinning. She ached for him, yet part of her was frightened, frightened by the very intensity of her own feelings. That his lovemaking would carry them both to the very pinnacle of ecstasy she had no doubt. *But when it was over, what then?*

He was due to leave in three weeks. It would be hard enough to say goodbye the way things were now. If she gave in to the fervent urgency his touch aroused, how would she ever cope with his going?

She wanted Brent with all her heart and soul. Her body craved his, a need as desperate as water in the dusty wastes of the Sahara. But without love, without commitment, the all-consuming flame would quickly die to ashes. And there was no love. How could there be? It was too soon. Love needed time and they had known each other only a few days. *And yet . . .*

'Laura?' he prompted.

'I . . . I can't.' She laughed unsteadily. 'Would you believe I've got to work late?'

He was silent for a moment, then gently but firmly, he held her at arm's length. 'You *have* to work, Laura?'

She searched his face, but his expression gave nothing away. Everyone she had ever loved had gone from her. First her father, then her mother. Gavin had his own life and would soon be married. She had trusted Jeremy and been betrayed. Brent would go away too. He had no choice, another job was waiting. If she made love with him, there would be no going back, she would fall *in* love with him. She could not afford that. Swallowing hard, she drew in a deep breath. 'I have to.'

'Are you afraid?' he asked softly. Avoiding his gaze she tried to pull free. His grip tightened. 'I want an answer.'

'Yes,' she blurted. 'Yes, I'm afraid.'

'So am I,' he cut in brusquely, and let her go.

Shocked, Laura didn't move. 'You?'

He raked his hair impatiently and, turning away, began pacing the office, finding release in physical activity for all his tension and frustration. 'Not of sex, I'm no monk. There have been other women.'

Laura coloured at his bluntness and experienced a moment's knifing jealousy that any other woman should have been loved by this tall, fiercely attractive man who was prowling the room with the feline grace and controlled power of a caged tiger.

'I mean *us*, you and me. I——' He shrugged and she glimpsed once more the vulnerability she had sensed that first morning. 'I want you, Laura. I'd be a liar to pretend otherwise. No other woman has ever got to me the way you do. But it's more than that. I—oh, *hell*,' he muttered violently, revealing something of his emotional turmoil, as the door opened and Jeremy walked in.

His smile of satisfaction at seeing Laura faded as he caught sight of Brent. He seemed to sense the charged atmosphere for his gaze swivelled between the two.

Concerned as she was for Brent, Laura did not miss the sudden rush of jealousy, swiftly masked, that swelled in Jeremy's eyes and suffused his face with ugly colour.

'Here *again*, Lewis? This office seems to hold a peculiar fascination for you. But while we all like to assist the Press,' he fastened Laura with his pale gaze, 'I do have a business to run. I'm sure you understand.'

All emotion was wiped from Brent's face, leaving it bleak and cold. He opened his mouth, but before he could speak, Jeremy turned to Laura. 'Have you prepared the report and list I asked for?'

She dragged stricken eyes from Brent. 'Not yet,' she began. 'I was just——'

'Then we had better go through it together.' His smile reminded her of a shark, cold-blooded and totally without humour. 'Business before pleasure. No doubt Lewis will excuse us.' Perching on the corner of her desk, he turned his back on Brent and from that moment behaved as though he was no longer there.

'I had a long chat with Luke Callero this afternoon. Charming chap, my kind of man.'

While Jeremy, basking in a glow of self-satisfaction, burbled on about all he had in common with the head of the Callero business empire, Laura risked a quick glance at Brent, and almost wished she hadn't.

Was that accusation in his eyes? Eyes that were as hard and black as jet. Surely he realised she didn't *want* to be stuck here, with Jeremy of all people? He must know that, despite her nervousness, she would rather be with him. There was still so much they had to say to one another, still so much to learn. Just as he had lifted one corner of the curtain, permitting her a tantalising insight into how *he* felt, Jeremy had barged in. *Damn Jeremy Grainger.* Laura was startled at the force of her own feelings.

But what could she do? Jeremy was temporarily in overall charge. He had only just arrived. He had every right to ask her to work late, at least until he was conversant with everything relating to the project.

She tried desperately to convey this to Brent as she looked at him.

'I hope you are listening to me, Laura,' Jeremy said tartly.

She switched her gaze, angry that he should have noticed, and also at the warmth she could feel in her cheeks. 'Of course,' she said evenly.

'Only Luke is a little concerned about the way Dennis has been handling certain matters. Apparently one or two rather important people have had their feathers ruffled. Nothing I won't be able to smooth over,' he added, as she was about to protest. 'But I think you and I will have to come to a new arrangement about the way public relations is managed. By the way, Sam Lincoln is rather upset, annoyed is perhaps a better description, that you didn't bother to tell him about Dennis's illness.'

'I hardly had time,' Laura protested. 'I only found out——'

'You seem to have enough time for other things, other *less important* things.' Behind his smile, Laura could see bitterness and envy. 'I wonder, Laura, is your heart really in the job?' Her spirits sank. He hadn't even got into his stride yet. Depression settled over her like a heavy blanket.

'Let's go into my office.' It was a command, not a suggestion. He stood up and made a great play of surprise at seeing Brent still there.

'I'll tell you what, Lewis, you seem to have time on your hands and nothing much with which to fill it. Do me a favour and fetch us some coffee and sandwiches from that little café down the street.' Jeremy reached for a slim, pig-skin wallet and extracted a ten-pound note.

Laura blanched, and held her breath. *He was treating Brent as an errand boy.*

'Have something yourself if you like. Can't ask you to join us, I'm afraid. With so much to do,' he moved narrow shoulders under the expensive cloth, 'you know how it is.'

'I know exactly how it is,' Brent replied in a voice that made Laura think of the glinting edges of broken bottles.

Jeremy placed the note on the corner of Laura's desk, then looked at his gold Rolex and shook his head. 'At this rate it could be midnight before we're finished. Come along, Laura.' He started towards the connecting door.

Her nerves were as taut as violin strings. She took a step forward, stopping as she heard a sound behind her. If Brent involved himself it would only rebound on *him*, as well as her and Dennis. Jeremy would not be touched. She threw an anxious glance over her shoulder, silently warning, *pleading* with him to say nothing.

He stared at her for a long moment, then turned and walked out.

'Peculiar fellow,' Jeremy observed from the doorway. 'He didn't take the money.'

Laura gritted her teeth. 'I don't think he'll be coming back.'

'Maybe you'd like to run down for something?'

She looked steadily at him. 'No thank you, I'm not hungry.' The very thought of sharing food with him made her stomach heave.

'No? Oh, all right.' He leaned over the desk, checked the directory and picked up the phone. 'In that case, I'll just order for myself.'

For the next four hours, Laura was kept busy. She ignored the aroma of hot coffee and savoury sandwiches, ignored the pangs in her stomach, telling herself they were *not* hunger pains, simply the result of stress, which was at least partially true.

At least Jeremy's decision to have supper at his desk gave her an ideal excuse to return to her own office to prepare the report and list he wanted. He insisted on the connecting door remaining wide open, and frequently shouted through, wanting to know where various things were kept.

As soon as she had finished he started reading off a long list of queries relating to figures and correspondence. Much of it was straightforward, but there was one difficult moment concerning the finance. But she was able, with a silent and heartfelt prayer of thanks, to assure him that the funds for the next phase were already in the bank and a confirming letter on its way.

Almost all his questions were unnecessary, covering details he could easily have found out, or checked, for himself. But realising he already knew that and was out to prove a point, she hung on to her temper, kept silent, and did as she was asked.

And he made a point of *asking*. There were no commands or instructions. It was all *would you mind . . .* and *do you think you could . . .* Which somehow made it worse.

She very nearly exploded when he asked her to copy the daily results of the last two months' test drilling for the third time. But she had vowed, for Dennis's sake, to see the job through and *nothing* Jeremy Grainger did was going to change that.

So she answered his questions relating to the business with as much politeness as she could manage, ignored his compliments and flattery, and simply stared past him, blank-faced, or walked away, when he tried to sound her out about her relationship with Brent.

Those moments were hardest of all, for inside she was a mass of raw nerves and seething emotions.

It was almost eleven when she finished. There was not a single item on his list that had not been dealt with. There was no reason for her to stay a moment longer. She knew it, and she knew he did too.

'That's it, Jeremy. I'm going home now.' She announced with quiet finality.

'Let me get you a taxi.'

'No, thank you.' She replaced the last of the files and shut the cabinet.

'You must, I insist. In fact, I'll see you back to your hotel. It's the least——'

Laura turned on him. 'I will call my own taxi, and I will go home alone. We work for the same company, Jeremy. As far as I am concerned, that is the *only* link we have. And, by the way, as tomorrow is my normal day off, and there cannot possibly be anything more for me to do for at least forty-eight hours, I will not be coming in. Goodnight.' She marched into her own office to collect her personal belongings.

He followed her. The veneer had cracked and all the pent-up malice spilled out. 'You're wasting your time, you know. You'll never get anywhere with Lewis. Into his bed, perhaps, but that will be all. There isn't a woman born who can pin him down. Don't you know his reputation? God, he'd turn Casanova green with envy.'

Laura looked up briefly. 'And you too, Jeremy?'

He flushed, but her comment didn't stop him. 'Look at his lifestyle. He's never in the same country longer than a month. I'd bet a year's salary that he's got a different woman in every port.'

Laura clamped her lips together to prevent the hot denials spilling out.

But in the taxi, resting her head against the back of the seat, Jeremy's spiteful gibes came back to haunt her.

She thought of all she knew about Brent, of what Dennis had told her and what she had learned for herself. There was still so much she *didn't* know.

But then, how could she? They had been together such a short time. Yet, when he kissed her—the memory of his mouth on hers, his warm breath fanning her cheek, the knowing strength in his hands, fingers pressing against her spine—her heart kicked wildly and she closed her eyes, rolling her head against the seat.

How could she doubt him? From the moment they met there had been a special spark between them. And when they kissed and touched it threatened to flare into a conflagration, a holocaust which would devour them both. Could such passion be purely physical? *Surely not?*

Drooping with fatigue, she paid the driver and walked slowly up the steps and into the hall.

As she reached her door and opened it the phone started to ring. Closing the door, she stared at it. What if it was Jeremy? She could not take any more of him tonight. But it might not be. It could be anyone. Her gaze darted to the clock. *At this hour?*

Tossing her bag on to the table, she kicked off her shoes and snatched up the receiver. 'Hello?'

'It's me.' Brent's voice came down the line and Laura's eyes closed as, despite her weariness and the terrible strain of the day, her spirits soared. *It was wonderful to hear him.* She lay back on the pillows, pressing the receiver tightly to her ear.

'Hello, me. Have you been bribing the receptionist again?'

'I should have done. But he might have forgotten, or missed you. I've been calling your room every fifteen minutes since...well, never mind.' There was a pause. 'Everything OK?'

Laura discerned several shades of meaning in the apparently casual enquiry. She heard the echo of his anger, of his dislike and contempt for Jeremy. She also sensed uncertainty. But overlaying it all was deep and genuine concern.

Her gaze strayed to the rose, now in full, magnificent bloom, and she smiled. 'Apart from terminal exhaustion, I'm fine.'

He wasn't convinced. 'You're quite sure?'

'I can handle him, Brent,' she said quietly. *It's you I'm out of my depth with.*

'Does he want you in the office for the whole day tomorrow?'

She turned over on to her stomach. 'Actually, I'm not going in at all tomorrow. It's my day off. I wouldn't normally have taken it the way things are, but as Jeremy has been through everything with a fine-tooth comb, there'd be nothing for me to do except the day's post, and we're not expecting anything urgent.' She twisted a stray lock of hair round and round her finger. 'I expect you'll be interrogating some poor, defenceless company director,' she teased.

'As a matter of fact, I planned to work in my room for a couple of hours after breakfast, then take the rest of the day off.'

Excitement stirred in the pit of her stomach, but she hid it beneath gentle scepticism. 'Really?'

'Yes. As of ten seconds ago, that was exactly what I'd decided. I should be finished by ten-thirty. How about spending the rest of the day with me?'

She could think of nothing more wonderful, but...

'You could take me sight-seeing,' his deep voice sent shivers down her spine, 'force-feed me culture and history.'

'All right,' she agreed, and after a moment's hesitation, plunged on, 'where shall we meet?'

'Where would you suggest?' There was a hint of laughter in his tone and she knew he had guessed the cause of her brief uncertainty. If he came to her room...

'The foyer?' she suggested, glad he could not see her blush.

'Where else?' *He was still laughing.*

'I'll see you in the morning, then. Goodnight, Brent.'

'Goodnight, Laura. Laura, I——'

She waited. 'Yes?'

'We have a lot of talking to do.'

Her heart thumped, making her oddly breathless. 'Yes.'

'Sleep well.'

'You too.'

There was a click and the line went dead. Replacing the receiver, Laura swung her feet on to the floor and, singing happily to herself, got ready for bed.

CHAPTER EIGHT

AT ten twenty-five the following morning, Laura left her room. Fastening the zip of her white canvas bag, into which, as an afterthought, she had stuffed her swimsuit rolled up in a towel, she slung the strap over her shoulder and hurried down the passage, catching the lift just as the doors were closing.

Maybe she should have waited a little longer, been a few minutes late, for appearances' sake. She grinned to herself, bending her head so that the other two people in the lift, a silent-middle-aged couple, would not think she had entirely taken leave of her senses.

Appearances be blowed! This was the first day off she had spent with another person since coming to Gibraltar. And as that person was Brent Lewis, she had no intention of wasting a single, precious second.

She had dressed, feeling ridiculously excited, in white canvas jeans, sandals, and a loose-knit sweater in mint and white stripes over a cotton shirt. And, as a concession to the holiday mood, after brushing her hair thoroughly, she had left it to tumble in gleaming tawny waves about her shoulders.

Cool and fresh from the shower, replete with a good breakfast, she stepped out of the lift. Her cheeks were glowing and her eyes sparkled in anticipation of the day to come.

As she started across the foyer, Brent emerged from the little shop selling newspapers and confectionery, tucking some bars of chocolate into a navy nylon rucksack which he then hitched over one shoulder. He stopped as he saw her and slowly studied her from head to toe.

She stood quite still, her breathing constricted, and felt her colour rise at the warmth and approval in his gaze.

'You look . . . wonderful,' he said as he reached her.

Trying to contain her brimming joy was not easy. She leaned back and, in playful mockery, surveyed him as he had her.

His faded jeans outlined powerful thighs, and a pale blue sweat shirt, the sleeves pushed half-way up arms burned bronze beneath the dark hair, clung to his heavily-muscled shoulders. The devil-may-care light in his brown eyes was reflected in his crooked grin. It sent a frisson along her nerves.

'You don't look too bad yourself,' she forced the grudging note into her voice. In fact, he took her breath away.

'Gee, thanks, lady. You ready to go some place now?' The accent was pure Bronx, and so unexpected it sent Laura into a fit of giggles. 'Where on earth did you pick that up?'

He drew his upper lip over his teeth, Bogart-style. 'I bin around, kid.'

Laura shook her head, intrigued.

'Actually,' he said coolly, reverting to normal speech, 'it's just one of my many talents.'

'I can't wait to see the others,' she grinned.

He raised one eyebrow. 'Oh, you will,' he threatened. 'You will. Now, hand in your key and let's get moving.'

As she dropped the key on the desk, Inez emerged from the office. Observing Laura, her face alight with happiness, and Brent grinning close behind her, Inez smiled.

'Have a nice day,' she called after them, and was clearly bemused by their simultaneous laughter as they waved to her before disappearing through the main doors and down the steps.

Brent caught Laura's hand. 'I don't suppose it crossed your mind to bring a swimsuit?'

She patted her bag. 'Of course.'

He whistled. 'The girl has brains as well. Right, lead on. But before we start, can I suggest that we do all the heavy stuff this morning and leave decisions about this afternoon until after lunch?'

Laura shrugged easily. 'That's fine by me.' She shot him a sidelong glance. 'Copping out already, eh?'

'Not at all. But this,' he squeezed her hand, 'is a special day and, much as I am looking forward to learning about this fascinating lump of rock, I also want time to pursue enquiries of a more... personal nature.'

Laura looked down, her warm flush of excitement pierced by a tremor of apprehension.

'Well?' Brent goaded. 'What are we waiting for?'

They went first to the museum, and as they wandered through the rooms and down below to the fourteenth-century Moorish bath-house Laura found her mind operating on two levels. Part of her was thoroughly enjoying guiding him around the displays which brought to life Gibraltar's history through the ages. She relished being able to give him little extra snippets of information, especially about the original port area, which she had picked up from her own reading, and meetings with local people. He teased her about her 'rag-bag' memory, but she could see he was impressed and his admiration kindled a warm glow inside her.

The other half of her was keenly aware of his hand holding hers, the pressure of his strong fingers, his warm breath fanning her cheek as they leaned over an exhibit together, and the brush of arm, thigh or chest against hers.

All her senses were alive to him. She could smell the musky fragrance of his aftershave, sandalwood soap and the clean, soap-powder scent of his sweatshirt. She was captivated by the warmth and texture of his skin, and the fine lines at the corners of his eyes which deepened when he smiled. His voice enthralled her. Its deep, rich timbre and slow cadences sent delicious shivers down her spine, especially when he leaned close to murmur remarks about some of the items on display.

They moved on to the tree-lined piazza, where flower-sellers displayed buckets full of white, yellow and scarlet blooms.

'Where would you like to go next?' Laura asked, one hand holding wind-tousled hair off her face. The breeze was quite strong and though all around the Rock the sky was clear, above the town one heavy cloud obscured the sun and Laura was glad of her sweater.

'Tempt me,' he suggested, the corners of his mouth lifting.

'Well, as you're really into history,' Laura smiled blandly, glad he could not see her quickening heart-beat, 'we could go to Casemates Square, where they used to hold public hangings, or to the law courts in Main Street, where the case of the *Marie Celeste* was heard. Then again, we could go to Rosia Bay and see the Rock Buster.'

His heavy brows lifted. 'What's *that*?'

'A gun,' she replied. 'It dates from 1884 and weighs one hundred tons. It had a range of eight miles which, in those days, was pretty remarkable. The only trouble was, it took thirty-five men two hours to get it ready to fire, and as each shell weighed two thousand pounds, they could only fire one round every four minutes. Even so,' she shuddered, 'I wouldn't like to have been on the receiving end.'

'Rosia Bay is quite a walk,' Brent said, 'is there nothing nearer?'

'My, don't you tire easily,' Laura gibed.

But he came back, quick as a flash. 'Not at all, I'm simply conserving my energy. I told you, I have other, more demanding ideas in mind for later.' And as she floundered for an adequate retort, he went on, 'Let's go and see the castle. I like castles. I have a lot of sympathy with the knights of old who, when their women gave them any trouble, used to lock them up for a week or two, to bring them to their senses.'

'I *was* right,' Laura stood, arms akimbo, hands on her hips, 'you *are* a chauvinist.'

His eyes narrowed as he turned to her, and her heart raced as he brought his face down within an inch of hers, but she didn't flinch. 'Only when driven to it,' he murmured in mock threat.

'Oh, Grandmama, what a short fuse you have.' Laura rounded her eyes innocently.

Suppressing his grin, Brent grated, 'Get up that hill before I make an exhibition of us both.'

Hand in hand they climbed to the remains of the vast Moorish castle whose walls had once enclosed an area reaching almost to the sea. The hillside was dominated by the massive square tower.

Brent tilted his head back to look up at the pale stone walls, pocked with age and the scars of battle. 'Do you know when it was built?' As she opened her mouth to reply, he grinned and murmured, 'Stupid question.'

Laura glared at him, but couldn't help grinning back. 'The original castle dates back to the year 711, when Tarik Ibn Ziad first conquered Gibraltar and gave it his name.' Gooseflesh erupted on her arms as she recalled her nightmare and, unconsciously, she rubbed them as Brent watched her while he listened.

She moistened her lips and looked up at the castellated tower.

'That was the beginning of a war between Moslems and Christians which lasted nearly eight hundred years. King Ferdinand of Castile and Leon recaptured the Rock in 1309, but the Moors took it back in 1333 and held it for the next hundred and twenty-nine years. The main keep had been so badly damaged, they rebuilt it into the present Tower of Homage.'

He gazed at the tower once more. 'It certainly looks pretty solid.'

She nodded. 'It is. In fact, apart from four small rooms at the top, it's a solid mass of masonry. I think they call it *tapia*, it's a mixture of pebbles and concrete. During that siege, the poor Spaniards defending it almost starved to death. All they had left to eat was the leather from their belts, shields and shoes.'

They climbed the stairs to the exhibition and spent over half an hour among the life-sized models of the personalities originally connected with the tower.

Dark-skinned, mostly bearded, and clothed in the richly-embroidered robes of the period, they kindled in Laura a strong sense of history. Allowing her thoughts free rein, she imagined them planning the siege, discussing strategy, details of attack and defence, and the most effective use of men and weapons.

Surreptitiously, she watched Brent as he studied the tall, swarthy figure of Tarik Ibn Ziad, whose long sword was held at his waist by a length of saffron cloth. A breastplate covered the top half of his white robe and a long, scarlet cloak was flung back from one shoulder.

Once more, despite the comfort of her sweater, her skin grew cold as she compared the long-dead conqueror with the tall, dark man to whom she was in mortal danger of losing her heart.

Who would have won, she mused, had these two ever confronted one another?

Brent moved, and she looked away.

Close by stood the slender figure of an Arab princess, clad in a long, full-sleeved gown of pale blue belted with an embroidered cord. Her black hair hung down her back and was covered with a white cloth. Beside the Moor she looked delicate and ethereal. Their heads were turned towards one another and, as Laura gazed at them, Brent murmured in her ear, 'Were they lovers, do you think?'

She started. 'I—I don't know.'

'Perhaps she was his wife. Or one of them. The laws of Islam allow a man four, don't they?'

'Only if he can promise to treat each one equally in every way,' she replied at once. 'I wouldn't think there are many men who could live up to that kind of pressure.'

'Oh, I don't know,' he countered and, as she turned to argue, he raised one dark brow and she realised he was poking gentle fun at her.

'Lunch?' she suggested sweetly.

'How about a swim first?'

She gestured to the scrub and stunted trees surrounding them on the rocky hillside. 'Did you have anywhere in mind?'

He nodded. 'Yes,' he said quietly, his grin fading. 'The beach where we danced.' Their eyes met and her heart contracted painfully. *Oh, God, it would be so easy to fall in love with him*. She tore her gaze away, pretending to look at the view. She mustn't even *think* it. It was a joy to be with him, to laugh and tease, to show him the sights, and share with him the fascination of this unique place. He understood the demands of her work, as she did his, but it was an interlude, nothing more. He would

move on and she...she would miss him more than she
dared contemplate.

'What a smashing idea,' she said with forced
brightness. 'But not on that beach, I'm afraid. The red
flag will be flying.'

He looked nonplussed. 'Why?'

'Because of the wind,' she explained. 'They call it the
Levanter. It whips up huge waves and makes swimming
on the eastern side too dangerous. Look,' she pointed
upwards, 'you see that cloud, hanging just above the
peak. That's caused by the Levanter wind.'

He followed her pointing finger. 'How?'

'The warm, moist air is driven against the steep side
of the Rock and forced upwards. As soon as it meets
the cooler air above, it condenses. You can actually stand
above the cloud and watch it forming. Would you like
to see?'

He shrugged and smiled. 'Why not? But let's eat first.'

Laura decided to pay him back for his teasing. 'Getting
to you, is it? All this fresh air and culture? Are you
missing the clatter of typewriter keys? The feel of a pen
gripped in your fingers as you prise information from
yet another hapless victim?'

He gave a slow, lazy smile that made Laura tingle from
the roots of her hair to her toenails. 'Not at all. Just
keeping my strength up. After all, who knows what the
rest of the day may bring. We've barely got started.'

Aware that somehow he had won this exchange as well,
Laura darted ahead of him down the hill, his deep-
throated chuckle floating after her.

The little bar-cum-restuarant was almost full. Above
the polished wood counters hung hams and sausages,
ropes of garlic and peppers, and sides of dried salt
codfish. Waiters with large trays laden with plates and
bowls containing many different and colourful dishes

squeezed between the closely packed round tables. The air was filled with music and chatter, the chink of cutlery and glasses and the aroma of spicy food.

'Have you had *tapas* before?' Brent asked as he held her chair.

Laura shook her head. 'What is it?'

'They,' he corrected. 'They are really appetisers, a range of several dishes of meat, fish, vegetables, eggs and so on, but served in very small portions, so that you can have several different things instead of one main course. You eat from as many, or as few, as you like. Trust me?' he added, as a waiter hovered ready to take their order.

She grinned wryly. 'Do I have a choice?'

He threw her a look that curled her toes, and ordered puff-pastries filled with spiced meat, stuffed mushrooms, potato salad with capers, egg plant and tomatoes, and avocado stuffed with shrimp, plus chilled white wine for her and iced lager for himself.

'We'll never eat all that,' she gasped as the waiter hurried away.

'Wait until it arrives, you'll be surprised.'

As the waiter unloaded the dishes, Laura's mouth began to water. All the portions, beautifully presented, were tiny.

After a moment or two's shyness, she got used to the idea of taking a forkful at a time from each of the bowls and plates. She even found herself eating off Brent's fork as he selected some choice morsel she had never tasted before and insisted she try it.

To her surprise there was nothing she didn't like. 'Where do *tapas* come from?' she asked, sipping her wine.

'You mean you don't know?' he mocked.

She threw him a baleful glare.

'All right,' he raised one hand in surrender. 'The custom originated about a hundred years ago in the Andalucia region of Spain when slices of ham or sausage were placed over the mouths of glasses of sherry served before lunch or dinner.'

Laura speared another stuffed mushroom. 'Why are they called *tapas*? What does it mean?'

'Lids,' Brent replied succinctly, swallowing a mouthful of avocado and shrimp. 'It comes from the verb *tapar*, which means to cover.'

He silenced her offer to split the bill with an icy, withering glance that reminded her just how formidable an enemy he could be.

As they left the crowds and shops behind, passing tiny terraced gardens, and window boxes ablaze with scarlet geraniums, he spoke of his family home and of his parents' love of gardening.

'They inherited the house from my father's mother. It's Georgian.' His eyes softened at some memory. 'A wonderful place to grow up in. But after my brother and I had gone it was too much for them to manage on their own. We had a big family conference and suggested they move to somewhere smaller, but they refused. They couldn't face the thought of leaving the garden. He grimaced. 'There's five acres of it, plus an orchard and a beech wood.'

'What happened?' Laura asked shyly. He had never mentioned his family before. And while she was hungry to learn anything she could about him, she was well aware that he was an intensely private man. He was quite capable of slamming the door on any question he judged intrusive. Yet he had started the conversation, with no prompting at all from her.

He grinned. 'They stayed put. But things were a bit fraught for a while. The family solicitor had been concerned for some time about death duties, and wanted my parents to deed the property to my brother and me while they were still alive. The only trouble was, my brother didn't want it.'

Laura couldn't contain her amazement. *'What?'* she blurted. 'I'm sorry,' she said hastily, 'I shouldn't have——'

'It's all right, I was rather surprised myself. But apparently his wife wants a new house nearer London. Anyway, we eventually reached a compromise. Rob's a graphic designer and works from home, so he and Julia have offered to stay on to keep an eye on things until I can afford to buy them out. My parents are happy, and Rob and Julia are delighted.'

'And you?' she looked up at him.

His mouth twisted. 'I'd never imagined myself *a man of property*, I've always been on the move. For the last ten years home has been a hotel bedroom and whatever I could pack into a suitcase. At first I put it down to the demands of the job, then it grew to be a habit. 'I did nearly settle down once.' He stopped, his features bleak. 'But it didn't work out,' he finished briefly.

Cheryl, Laura thought with a pang.

'Sometimes,' he shrugged, 'the idea of roots and a settled life,' he held her gaze for a long moment, 'doesn't seem such a bad idea after all. What about you? I know you like roses.' They exchanged a smile. 'But have you got green fingers?'

Laura made a wry face. 'I've never had time to find out.' And she started to tell him something of her background. It was difficult at first, the memories were painful. But he seemed so genuinely interested, she found it easier by the moment. He listened, rarely interrupting except to prompt very gently when she strayed from the point or was uncertain whether or not to continue.

Almost without realising it she found herself telling him about the effect her father's death had had upon her mother.

'It seems a terrible thing to say, but sometimes I felt she hated him for what he'd done, for saving that little girl, because it had cost his own life.'

'And your mother was angry with him for leaving her,' Brent said. 'I'm told anger is a normal part of the grieving process. Apparently we have to go through several stages before we can fully come to terms with the loss of someone we love. Sadly, some people get stuck in one of the stages and never do accept what's happened. But people react in different ways. My grandmother, for instance.'

'What happened to her?' Laura asked. She was heedless of the dappled shadows as sunlight played through the whispering trees on either side of the narrow road. Lizards skittered across the sun-baked rock and hid among the plants and grasses.

She sensed he rarely talked like this. After all, in whom would he confide? He was always on the move, travelling alone. He was not the kind of man to open his heart to the bartender in his hotel after a couple of drinks.

'Nothing,' he said, 'she lived to be eighty-six and died peacefully in her sleep.'

Laura frowned, then shook her head uncertainly. 'I don't understand.'

He was silent for a moment as if collecting his thoughts. 'My grandfather was master of a small cargo boat that was lost with all hands off the Florida coast. My grandmother simply refused to accept that she would never see him again, even after wreckage bearing the ship's name had been washed ashore. She kept his clothes pressed and aired and refused to part with any of his personal possessions. She often talked about the things she would tell him when she saw him.' Brent glanced at Laura. 'Those were the words she always used, *when she saw him,* never *when he comes home.*'

Without breaking his stride or removing his arm from her shoulder, he snapped off a twig from an overhanging branch with his free hand, turning it round and round in his fingers as they continued up the hill.

She did not speak, knowing he would go on when he was ready. Instead, she slipped her arm loosely round his waist, offering silent comfort, and felt the acknowledging pressure from his fingers.

'My parents used to exchange meaningful looks and change the subject, but she would wink at me and smile, as though we had a secret that no one else shared, and carry on with her knitting. You see, she did know, but she had simply decided to treat his death as a longer voyage than usual. It was the only way she could cope. But there was never any doubt in her mind that they would meet again.'

Laura was silent for a moment. 'How old was she when your grandfather died?'

'Sixty-one.'

'But that means...' Laura started, then broke off, cringing at her own tactlessness. However, Brent didn't seem the least perturbed.

'Yes, she lived another twenty-five years. She was quite happy to join in the big family parties at Christmas, but equally happy on her own with a book or her knitting and the radio. There was a sort of peacefulness about her, as though once he'd gone, nothing could ever really touch her again.'

'That's the way my mother was,' Laura said painfully. 'No one could reach her. I wanted to help, to comfort her, even though I didn't fully understand what had happened. I was only a child, I couldn't give her what she needed.'

'No one could,' he said. His arm was warm, its weight comforting. 'Do you still blame yourself for that?'

She thought for a moment. 'No, not any more. For a long time I thought that there must have been something more I could have done, that I must have failed her in some way. I'd known other families where a parent had died, and it had drawn them closer together, but with us——' she turned her head away, fighting back tears '—except for my brother. Without him——'

'So, tell me about him,' Brent invited.

Laura swallowed hard. She looked up quickly. 'Why?'

He shrugged and smiled. 'Why not? He's your brother, so that makes him interesting.'

Brent slanted one dark brow. He seemed puzzled by her silence. 'Do you see him often?'

Laura shook her head. 'Not as often as I'd like. His main office is in London, but he travels to New York quite frequently. He phones or writes whenever he can and keeps me in touch with all that's going on in his life.'

'It sounds as though you're pretty close.'

She nodded. 'He was my best friend.'

'Was?'

'He's getting married very soon.' As the words left her lips she felt herself grow cold. 'Look, there's the cable-car station,' she said brightly, desperate to change the subject as quickly as possible. 'Oh, damn. It's not running.'

'We can walk up, can't we?' Brent suggested. 'If it's not too tiring for you.'

'I'll walk your legs off any time,' Laura retorted.

His slow smile was like feathers brushing her skin. 'How you love a challenge. OK, what's it to be then, up to the top and back via the Mediterranean Steps?'

Laura couldn't hide her dismay. 'But they go up over six hundred feet!'

'Get you every time, don't I?' he grinned.

'Oh, you——' As she thumped his chest he caught her hand and lifting it pressed a kiss on to her palm. His gaze held hers and she felt weak, as though she were melting inside. She lowered her eyes, afraid to look at him, afraid he would see how deeply he stirred her.

Releasing her hands, he put his arm around her shoulders again and, without speaking, they started up the road that zig-zagged to the peak.

As they climbed, the orchids and white narcissi gave way to palmetto, wild olive and eucalyptus. She pointed out the black kites and buzzards hovering above, swooping and soaring as they rode the wind, waiting for it to ease before they continued their migratory flight. Hundreds more squabbled for space on the slopes above and below the road. The noise was deafening.

They reached the gun emplacement at the top of the Rock, and Laura clung to the railings as the wind whipped her hair across her face.

'What a view,' Brent murmured as they gazed down at the panorama spread before them.

'Look.' Laura pointed. 'Can you see it?'

Below them and to their left, they could see the cloud forming. Like the steam from a million boiling kettles, it churned and swirled above their heads, yet instead of blowing away, it remained, as if anchored by invisible chains, hanging above and slightly to one side of the peak.

As the sun had moved around to the west, the cloud no longer cast its shadow over the town, and the buildings gleamed in the afternoon light.

Brent pointed to the enclosed bay almost directly below them. 'What's that place called?'

'Rosia Bay,' she almost had to shout. 'Nelson's body was landed there after the Battle of Trafalgar. It had been preserved in a barrel of rum. I'm told that ever since then, the Royal Navy has referred to the traditional tot as Nelson's blood.'

'That must be the Bay of Algeciras, and the Spanish mainland. And that,' he turned so that his chest was against her back, pointing over her shoulder across the straits towards the mountains on the horizon, 'that must be Africa.'

Laura twisted her head so he could hear her above the sound of the wind. 'The Atlas Mountains of Morocco. They're only fourteen miles away. You can fly to Tangier in twenty minutes.'

'And will you?' He folded his arm across the front of her chest, holding her against him as his lips touched her ear.

'Will I what?' She looked up at him.

'Fly to Tangier with me. Not this minute,' he added drily as her head jerked round and they bumped noses. 'Next week, on your day off. We could explore the Medina, the maze of alleys and shops where they sell everything from hand-beaten silver to charms against snake-bite. There are miles of empty beaches with fine white sand, and we could take a camel ride if you like.' He narrowed his eyes until they were merely glittering slits, and in a voice like gravel murmured, 'Come with me to the Casbah.'

Fighting to contain the laughter which dissolved her sudden tension, she stared up at him in mock horror. 'You're a white slaver!'

'Curses, you guessed.' He grinned. 'Come anyway. Please?'

Inwardly taking a deep breath, she nodded. 'I'd love to.'

His arm tightened and she felt a thrill of excitement. He lifted a handful of her hair and buried his face in it. 'It smells of sunshine and flowers,' he murmured, letting it spill through his fingers to be caught and tossed by the wind. 'Show me our beach.'

'It's——' She turned but he didn't move. She was facing him, their bodies touching. Swift, hot colour flooded her face, betraying the turmoil within. 'It's...' she swallowed, 'behind you,' she said huskily, refusing to meet his eyes. 'If you look down you'll see why we couldn't swim there today.'

He turned, drawing her close, reluctant, it seemed, to let her go, even for a moment.

The wind caught her hair, and it streamed back from her face like a flag.

Far below, mountainous seas with creamy crests thundered up the Mediterranean, crashing into fountains of spray on the empty sands. Laura moistened her lips. 'I taste all salty,' she exclaimed in surprise.

Brent glanced down. 'You do? Let's see.' Within the space of a heart beat his mouth was on hers, his lips warm, gentle and cherishing. One hand cupped her head, the other pressed, splay-fingered against her lower spine, moulding her to him.

She felt his body quicken as desire flared, a hungry flame, engulfing them both. The bitter-sweet ache of longing filled her and they were both breathing hard as he leaned his forehead against hers. 'Oh, Laura,' he muttered. And she knew in that moment that the battle was over, she could not fight it, or him, any more.

'Laura...I...' he began hoarsely.

She pressed her index finger to his lips. 'I know,' she whispered. 'Shall we go back now?'

He moved his head a fraction to stare at her. 'To the hotel?'

She nodded.

'Are you sure that's what you want?'

She smiled at him. 'Oh, yes,' she said softly, 'quite sure.'

This time his kiss was hard and fierce and, when at last he released her, her legs felt like jelly. Without speaking he clasped her hand tightly and led her towards the long flight of steps which would take them on to the lower road and back to town.

Half-way down Brent stopped, looking back over his shoulder to where she stood, a couple of steps above him. 'There's chocolate in my rucksack if you'd like some.'

'Mmmm, lovely.' Laura unbuckled the pocket. 'It seems ages since lunch.'

'We must keep our strength up.' Something in his tone made Laura dart a glance at him, only to find him already watching her. The infinitesimal lift of one dark eyebrow made her blush even as they exchanged a smile that made words superfluous.

'It is a long walk back,' she agreed.

'In fact,' he added, 'I can't imagine why we're wasting time here,' and taking one step back up, he planted a lingering kiss on her willing mouth.

As they continued down the steps he asked her about the plants and shrubs growing in rich profusion around them. Laura pointed out several dwarf fan palms, a prickly pear cactus, pink candytuft and the bright orange heads of red-hot pokers.

Once they reached the road, her heart began to beat a little faster. She had to admit it, she was nervous. She did not fear his awesome strength. Instinct told her he would be tender and gentle, at least until he was certain her desire matched his own. After that . . . she shivered.

He looked down at her. 'What's the matter?'

Her smile wavered. 'Nothing.'

He let go of her hand and put his arm around her. 'You're not afraid, are you?'

She rested her head against his shoulder, marvelling at his ability to sense her mood. 'Not of you.' It was the truth. It was herself she feared. Would she be able to hide the fact that she was falling in love with him? There was something else. Jeremy had been the first man in her life and there had been no one since.

'I'm . . . it's . . .' She shrugged helplessly.

For a moment he seemed puzzled, then his face cleared and his eyes softened with tender warmth. '. . . been a long time?' he supplied with an understanding that made her heart lurch.

She nodded, gratitude overcoming her embarrassment.

He traced the line of her jaw, then tilted her chin, forcing her to meet his eyes. A wry smile played at the corners of his mouth. 'Snap,' he murmured.

Laura blinked. 'But . . . the papers said . . .' She faltered into silence, flushing painfully at his expression. A car-horn blared impatiently behind them. Brent caught her in his arms and jumped to the side of the road. His smile was twisted.

'You shouldn't believe everything you read in the papers,' he chided.

'Not even when *you* write it?' She wondered about the anger and *hurt* that had blazed briefly in eyes which were still guarded.

'That's different.'

She kept her expression serious. 'Of course.'

He relaxed and Laura felt inexplicably relieved, aware only as it faded of the unspoken threat which had hung over them both.

'I suppose they do tend to exaggerate,' she admitted.

He gave a brief, hard laugh. 'If I had slept with half the women the gossip columnists would have you believe, I'd never have had time, or the energy, to work. Besides,' his tone altered, recovering its undertone of dry humour, 'I'm rather choosy about my women, so consider yourself fortunate.'

Laura's eyebrows shot up. 'You pompous, arrogant, egotistical...' she spluttered.

'Save the compliments for later,' he interrupted, 'people are staring.'

Dissolving into laughter, Laura shook her head. 'You really are...'

'I think we've just been through all that,' he grinned as they approached the hotel entrance.

'I was going to say *impossible*.'

'You'll never manage it, you know,' he warned.

'What?'

He brought his face down close to hers. 'To have the last word.'

She wrinkled her nose at him. 'But haven't you always said I love a challenge?'

'Will you pick up both keys while I see if the newsagent has got my copy of *Lloyd's List*?' he said as they entered the foyer.

She gave an exaggerated sigh. 'What did your last slave die of?'

'Boredom,' he retorted and, flashing her a grin, strode into the little shop.

Laura approached the desk. The door to the office was closed and, hearing voices, Laura guessed Inez was busy. She was not altogether sorry. Despite the banter, her nervousness was returning, and she was not ready, yet, to share her secret even with as kind and sympathetic a person as Inez.

As she picked up the keys the girl passed to her, she heard her name shouted and spun round to see her brother emerging from the lift.

For a split second she froze in utter horror. Then, his obvious delight at seeing her swept everything else aside. 'Gavin!' she cried, and flung herself into his arms, shrieking as he enveloped her in a bear-hug and swung her round.

'How's my favourite sister?' He set her down and held her away to look at her. His beaming smile threatened to split his narrow face in two. His sandy hair was as rumpled as usual but he looked well and very happy. 'Not bad, not bad at all.' His smile faded slightly. 'Though you're not exactly piling on the pounds, are you?'

'Didn't you know?' she responded at once. 'I'm very fashionable. It's the lean, athletic look. Anyway,' she said, quickly steering the subject to what was uppermost in her mind, 'what are you doing here so soon? I didn't expect you for weeks yet.'

He pushed his glasses up the bridge of his nose, a gesture she knew well from their childhood. 'Didn't I give you a date in my letter?' He looked puzzled. 'I'd have sworn I did. But we've both been so busy these past few months, and then with the wedding last week, it's quite possible I forgot. Look,' he seized her forearms, 'Cheryl will be down any minute.' He broke off, shaking his head in wonderment, a bemused grin on his face. 'Oh, Laura, she's a fantastic person. She's got looks, she's got talent and she loves me. I'm so lucky.'

Laura's heart contracted. 'So is she, she's got you.' She was so glad for him, yet second by second her tension was mounting.

'Come and have a coffee with us. No, better still, we'll crack a bottle of champagne and have a proper celebration.'

Laura flinched as an arm encircled her shoulders and she looked up quickly to see Brent, who, judging by his cool, quizzical expression, had just caught Gavin's last words.

Her nervousness was of a different kind now, and threatened, as each second passed, to explode into panic.

'What are you celebrating, Laura?'

She was so concerned with the terrible inevitability of what was about to happen, she was hardly aware of the undertone of possessiveness, *of jealousy*, in Brent's voice.

She swallowed. Her throat was dry. 'Not me.' She wondered in mild hysteria if she would ever have cause to celebrate anything again. 'This is my brother. He's the one who's celebrating.'

Why had she and Brent come back at precisely this moment? Why hadn't Gavin waited for Cheryl upstairs? Two minutes, that was all it would have taken to avert the disaster rushing towards them. No, it wouldn't, it would only have postponed it. With them all on the Rock at the same time, confrontation was inevitable, sooner or later.

Gavin offered his hand to Brent. 'I've just got married. Last week, actually.'

Brent shook the proffered hand, his manner visibly thawing. 'My congratulations.' He glanced down at

Laura in mild surprise. 'You never mentioned that your brother and his wife were coming to Gibraltar.'

Her tongue seemed glued to the roof of her mouth. 'Gavin hadn't—the date—I wasn't sure exactly——' Her words trailed off as his face clouded, his brows drawing together in a deepening frown.

'Gavin? *Gavin Jefford?*'

With a terrible, sickening certainty Laura knew then that her fears had been justified.

'That's me.' Gavin grimaced at his sister. 'Honestly, Laura, you might have introduced us properly.'

'I'm sorry,' she croaked, 'I——' She caught her breath as the lift doors opened.

Gavin turned, his face lighting up as a statuesque red-head emerged, head bent, rummaging in her bag. She wore a pink cotton flying-suit that should have clashed horribly with her colouring, but somehow didn't. Her hair was a glossy copper cap, falling from a centre-parting into a short, geometric style, and freckles dotted her creamy skin.

'Ah, here she is.' Gavin's pride was transparent. 'Darling, I want you to meet my sister Laura, and...' He glanced back at Brent, whose features looked as if they had been carved from solid stone. 'Sorry, I didn't catch your name.'

CHAPTER NINE

LAURA closed her eyes, her last desperate hope extinguished. There could be no doubt now. The expression on Brent's face said it all. Cheryl, Gavin's new wife, was indeed Brent's ex-fiancée. Each second seemed to drag with agonising slowness as she waited.

Brent took his arm from her shoulders and she was suddenly cold. 'Lewis,' he said, his deep voice empty of all expression. 'Brent Lewis.'

Cheryl's head jerked up. The colour drained from her face, leaving her freckles standing out like splashes of gold paint on white paper. 'You!' she whispered.

Gavin's gaze flew from Brent to Cheryl and back again. His smile faded and he drew closer to his wife. 'Is this——'

She nodded sharply, once.

Laura watched a dull angry flush spread over her brother's features.

The tense, shocked silence was broken by Brent. 'If you'll excuse me.' He turned away.

Automatically, Laura put out a hand to stop him, but recoiled and withdrew it swiftly as he raked her with a glance that seared and froze at the same time.

'*Trust,*' he spat for her ears alone. 'I should have known better.' Disdaining to wait for the lift, his mouth a thin, bitter line, he strode to the swing-doors leading to the stairs.

Gavin put his arm protectively around his wife. 'I'm sorry, love. I had no idea *he* would be here.'

She shook her head and the glossy hair swung like a satin curtain. 'It's all right, really.' She smiled reassuringly at him. 'It was just a bit of a shock, that's all. He was the last person I expected to see.' She turned apologetically to Laura. 'I'm so sorry. Shadows from the past...' She made a gesture as if to brush it all aside, then extended a slender, long-fingered hand. 'I'm Cheryl Parker...Jefford,' she corrected quickly, darting a guilty look at Gavin. 'Sorry, darling, I haven't quite got used to it yet.'

Laura mumbled a greeting. She desperately wanted to get away, to find Brent and explain.

'What is he doing here anyway?' Gavin demanded.

Laura dragged her attention back to her brother. 'What? Oh, working.' Her throat was stiff with dread. Why had he looked at her like that? Surely he couldn't blame *her*?

'Then what were you doing out with him?'

'Gavin,' Cheryl chided, 'Laura's not on trial.'

He shrugged uncomfortably. 'No, of course not. Sorry. It was just—that man caused Cheryl a lot of grief.'

'It's all right,' Laura said quickly. 'I understand, really.' And she did. Nothing would ever be the same for Gavin and herself. His loyalties had changed. Cheryl came first now. That was as it should be, but Laura had never felt so lonely. 'He's been writing a profile of our company and a project we're involved in. I was asked to show him around.'

'Ah,' Gavin nodded, 'so it's business.'

Laura swallowed. It had started out that way. 'Yes.'

'Only I wouldn't like to think of you getting tangled up with a man like that.'

'Gavin,' Cheryl poked him in the ribs, 'Laura's a big girl now. I'm sure she's quite capable of taking care of herself. Now, what about that drink you promised me?'

He kissed the top of her nose, which was level with his own. 'For you,' he said softly, 'anything.' He turned to Laura. 'Come on, sis, you must know all the right places. Let's go somewhere really nice and catch up on all the news.'

Laura saw Cheryl's smile falter a fraction and made a huge effort to smile naturally. 'You're on your honeymoon, Gavin. The last thing either of you needs is someone else tagging along. You'll be here for a few days, won't you?'

He exchanged a brief glance with Cheryl, then he said, 'Well, perhaps not quite as long as we thought. Under the circumstances...' He let the sentence trail off.

'Not to worry. We'll have plenty of time to catch up, but right now I'm dying for a shower and a change of clothes.' Her brittle façade began to crack. 'It's been a long day.'

'Have dinner with us then,' Gavin commanded. 'No arguments, it's all settled.' He hugged Cheryl. 'Come along, wife, let's go and find a beautiful sunset and some chilled champagne.'

Cheryl grimaced at Laura. 'Her master's voice,' she quipped. 'Lovely to meet you. See you later.'

Laura lifted her hand in farewell, watching as they went towards the entrance, arms around each other's waists, their heads close. Then she hurried to the lift.

In her room, Laura sat on her bed and stared at the phone. The rose had begun to droop and a single petal had fallen off.

All right, so it had been a shock for him, coming face-to-face with his ex-fiancée. But why had he reacted so harshly? Why had he turned on *her*?

It couldn't matter to him that Cheryl was married to someone else. *Unless he still felt something for her.* But

that didn't make sense. If he had cared that much, he
wouldn't have left her.

She reached out to pick up the receiver, but pulled her
hand back. What would she say? The bitter contempt
in his final glance before walking away had severely
shaken her as had his remark about trust. *She didn't
understand*. She needed time to sort out her thoughts,
and decide how best to approach him. Getting up from
the bed, she went to run a bath.

There were still a few sun-worshippers stretched out on
loungers around the rooftop pool, but only one person
was swimming.

Brent knifed through the azure water, using every
ounce of power in his muscles as he drove himself to the
limits of his strength. He counted four strokes for every
breath, concentrating on the numbers, refusing to permit
any other thought to enter his mind. Back and forwards
he went, length after length, as if the rhythmic working
of arms and legs could expunge the shock, and the
burning sense of betrayal. *She must have known all along
and she had said nothing.*

Naked, Laura slipped her robe on and started back to
the bathroom. She hesitated, the phone drawing her like
a magnet. If they could just break the ice, establish
contact, the rest would come. It wouldn't be easy. He
was obviously deeply angry, or hurt, or both. But unless
they talked, it would never be sorted out, and she simply
could not bear their relationship to end like this.

Before doubts could crowd in and change her mind
again, she snatched up the receiver. Sitting on the edge
of the bed, her voice tremulous, she asked for his room.
She was clasping the phone so tightly, her fingers ached.

She heard it ring, and moistened lips that were suddenly paper-dry. She waited, hardly daring to breathe.

After the tenth ring, Laura realised he wasn't going to answer. Replacing the receiver very carefully, she went slowly back to the bathroom.

As the light faded and the sky turned to pink and gold, Brent sat alone in the deserted pool area, a towel round his shoulders, his face buried in his hands, waiting for his breathing to return to normal.

Laura's watch showed it was nearly seven. Over two hours and no word. She leaned forward, staring into the mirror, and dusted more blusher on to her cheekbones in an effort to counteract her pallor. Only her love for her brother and her desire not to spoil the evening for Cheryl and him had persuaded her to join them for dinner. At least she could be certain of one thing, Brent's name would not be mentioned.

This was not the evening she had envisaged. 'Oh, Brent,' she whispered, throwing her head back as her eyes filled. She bit her lip and swallowed hard. She must not let go now. If she went down to dinner with red eyes, Gavin would not rest until he got the truth out of her. Yet what could she say? *I'm in love with the man who ditched the girl you've just married, and he's walked out on me too?*

Laura closed her eyes, digging her nails into her palms. It was like a black farce. *So why wasn't she laughing?*

The sound of the phone made her spin round, her eyes wide, heart racing. *Please—it had to be...* She snatched up the receiver. 'Yes?' Her voice was a strangled croak.

'See you in the bar in five minutes,' Gavin's voice, chirpy as a cricket, was loud in her ear. All the hope, all the excitement and surging happiness drained away, leaving her cold and empty. 'Laura? Are you there?'

She pulled herself together. 'Yes. Yes, that's fine Gavin.'

'Are you all right?' His concern came clearly down the line. 'You sound a bit odd.'

She clamped her hand over the mouthpiece and took a deep, shuddering breath. 'Of course I'm all right. Never better. See you downstairs.' She put the phone down quickly.

Though she drank rarely, and then only a glass of wine, Laura found herself longing for a brandy. Something to counteract the chill of shock and soothe the jagged edges of her pain.

Brent Lewis didn't want her. He wasn't even prepared to give her the chance to explain.

She sucked in a deep breath and squared her shoulders. She would just have to live with it. At least she had found out in time, *before* they had made love. For if this had happened after, how would she have borne it?

She compressed her lips hard to stop them trembling. She would never know now how it would have been, if the reality would have matched all her wild imaginings. She pressed her fingers to her temples.

After a few moments she straightened up and made a last check of her appearance. Gavin would dismiss the feverish light in her eyes as excitement. Her hair was swept up and secured by two combs, her make-up flawless, if a shade heavier than usual. She had put on the first dress that came to hand, a straight-skirted shirt-waist of peach silk crêpe de Chine.

Clipping on pearl earrings, she tucked a clean handkerchief and her lipstick into her cream purse, and picked up her key. Switching off the light, she went out, locking the door behind her.

*   *   *

Brent stepped out of the shower and fastened a towel around his hips. Using another to rub his hair dry, he padded barefoot into the bedroom. She must have had a reason for not telling him. She wasn't the kind of girl to cheat or lie.

So she says, his cynical self threw back at him.

She's not, he argued.

How do you know what she is? How long have you known her?

He hooked the towel around his neck and stood, unmoving, glaring at the phone. Why hadn't she rung?

You were the one who walked away.

What's the matter with her. Doesn't she care?

Do you?

Dammit, of course I do. No woman has ever got to me the way she does.

You want her, is that it?

Yes, I want her. But it's more, much more than that. I . . . I think I'm falling in love with her.

Does she know that?

I haven't spelled it out, but she must have some idea. The way things are when we're together, the way we tease, the way me make one another feel, she must *know.* I've told her things I normally never talk about.

And she listened, really listened, and then, without a word of explanation, you walked away.

With a muffled curse, Brent strode forward and picked up the receiver.

As Laura stepped into the lift, in her empty room the phone began to ring. She had reached the ground floor and was half-way across the foyer before it stopped.

Cheryl was perched on a bar stool and Gavin stood beside her, leaning on one elbow as they talked and laughed together.

Laura's envy was as sharp and piercing as a stiletto. Wanting only to return to her room, and hide from their happiness, she forced herself forward.

Gavin caught sight of her and straightened up. 'At last,' he beamed. 'Still, it was worth the wait.'

Laura stretched her mouth into a smile. They appeared to have put the whole dreadful incident out of their minds. 'Thank you, kind sir.' She turned to Cheryl who was wearing harem pants and a camisole top in a rich shade of turquoise. Slung around her shoulders was a loose-fitting jacket of fine, cream wool. 'I love your outfit. Is it one of your own designs?'

Cheryl's face lit up and she nodded. 'When I'm working I spend most of my time in jeans and a sweater, but,' she threw a warm, loving glance at Gavin, 'this was a wonderful opportunity to indulge myself a little.'

'She's such an excellent advertisement for her own talent,' Gavin added enthusiastically. 'It's great for business.'

'You intend to go on working, then?' Laura said.

'Oh, yes.' Cheryl nodded again. 'I'm only just beginning to make my name. I have so many ideas for new designs I can't get them down on paper fast enough.'

'We're going to concentrate on couture stuff for the next couple of years, aren't we, darling,' Gavin said proudly, 'then we're thinking of branching out into the upper bracket of the High Street chains with ready-to-wear.'

Laura's brows rose. 'We?'

'Gavin is going to take over the financial and marketing side of the business,' Cheryl explained, 'which will leave me free to concentrate on design.'

'It's an ideal partnership,' Gavin gazed adoringly at his wife. 'With Cheryl's talent and my financial expertise, plus contacts in Europe and New York, we'll be millionaires in no time, you wait and see.'

Laura smiled. 'I'd drink to that, if I *had* a drink, that is.'

Gavin groaned. 'Sorry, sis. What's it to be? No, on second thoughts, we'll stick to the bubbly. That's the only possible drink for an occasion like this.'

Laura raised her second glass, making all the right responses as Gavin and Cheryl talked, and wondered when the sparkling liquid would begin to dull the ragged edge of her misery.

'So *there* you are. I knew I'd find you sooner or later if I kept looking. And celebrating too, by the look of it.'

Laura froze as Jeremy's voice, loud and hearty, carried across the quiet hum of conversation. Whatever god she had offended was certainly exacting a cruel revenge.

'That's Grainger, isn't it?' Gavin hissed in her ear. 'What's he doing here? I thought you said he was in Rotterdam.'

'He was,' Laura murmured. 'But he was posted here a couple of days ago to replace my boss who's ill.' She had just finished her explanation when Jeremy reached them, immaculately groomed in a smart suit, every golden hair in place. His pale eyes, sharp and assessing, were at odds with his wide, friendly grin, and his gaze flickered swiftly over each of them in turn.

'So, may I ask what the occasion is? Though finding myself in the company of two such beautiful women is, for me, more than enough reason to celebrate.'

Cheryl caught Laura's eye and one beautifully arched brow lifted a fraction.

Jeremy turned to Gavin and thrust out his hand. 'I'm sure we've met before. Your face is very familiar.'

As Gavin's hand was seized and pumped, Laura said drily, 'This is my brother, Jeremy. You met in London.'

'Of course,' Jeremy gushed, 'how are you? It's marvellous to see you again.' But his eyes remained watchful. 'And this lovely lady?' He turned to Cheryl and raised her hand to his lips.

Laura didn't know whether to laugh or be sick.

'My wife,' Gavin replied. 'Cheryl, darling, this is Jeremy Grainger. He and Laura work together.'

'Mr Grainger.' Cheryl retrieved her hand. Her smile was polite but held little warmth.

'Actually, I'm Laura's boss,' Jeremy confided with an arch grin, 'but on social occasions we dispense with rank and just enjoy ourselves.'

Laura almost choked on her drink. *The smarmy hypocrite.*

'May I ask, is this a business trip or are you on holiday?' Jeremy enquired, rubbing his hands expectantly.

'We're on holiday,' Gavin replied, then his pride and happiness overflowed. 'Actually, Cheryl and I have just got married.'

Jeremy spread his arms wide. 'You're on your *honeymoon*? Well, no wonder you're celebrating.' He beckoned the bartender over. 'Another bottle of champagne.'

They watched as he drew the cork with a loud pop. First he filled Gavin and Cheryl's glasses, then turned to Laura. She shook her head, but he overrode her protest. 'No backsliding, you must toast the happy couple,' adding in a low mutter, 'this could have been us, Laura. It still could be if only you'd come to your senses and see reason.' He turned away, filling his own glass.

What did it take to get through that cast-iron ego? Laura wondered.

Jeremy raised his glass. 'Wishing you both health, wealth and great happiness.'

He sounded so *sincere*. As he tried to catch her eye, Laura deliberately turned away and found herself looking at Brent who was watching them from the far side of the room, his face an icy mask.

'Well, this has been marvellous,' Jeremy drained his glass, 'but I'm afraid it's back to business. Laura, I hate having to mention this——'

'Then don't,' she cut him off, setting her glass down with such force and haste that the champagne slopped over the side and formed a pool on the bar top. 'This is my day off.' Visibly startled, he gaped at her. She turned to her new sister-in-law. 'Cheryl, forgive me, I have to go, there's someone I really must see. Gavin,' she squeezed his arm, 'I'll explain later. Have a lovely meal.' Without a word or a glance at Jeremy, she whirled away, hurrying through the maze of tables and out into the foyer.

Brent was nowhere to be seen. His expression was etched in her memory and she stood, helpless, wondering which way he had gone.

Two hours later she had walked the length of Main Street. She had peered into every bar, every café, restaurant and nightclub, without so much as a glimpse of him. She had phoned the hotel twice and asked for his room, just in case he had returned. She had no idea what she would have said had he answered. But he didn't.

Almost weeping with tiredness and frustration, Laura began to feel slightly dizzy, and knew that if she didn't eat soon she would faint. Though her stomach ached for food, the thought of eating nauseated her. Yet how else could she continue her search?

She found a quiet café and forced down a cup of coffee and a toasted sandwich, determinedly ignoring the glances her solitary status attracted.

She could feel her strength returning with every mouthful. He must be somewhere in the city. Why couldn't she find him? As she got up to leave it suddenly hit her. *Of course.* Why hadn't she thought of it before? She tried to control the hope welling up inside her but, like steam, it would not be contained.

Paying her bill, she hurried out into the street, waving frantically at a passing taxi. It stopped in a squeal of brakes and tyres and backed up level with her. As she blurted out her destination, the driver's forehead creased in perplexity.

'You *sure* that's where you want to go?'

'Yes,' Laura nodded urgently, 'quite sure. Please hurry.' She climbed in. The driver shrugged and shook his head. Laura sat back, gripping her purse tightly. This was her last hope. If he wasn't there—she caught her lip between her teeth. He *had* to be. There was nowhere else left for her to try.

The taxi stopped and she climbed out. The wind tore at her hair, wrecking the elegant upswept style. Laura pulled the restraining combs out and shook it loose.

She stood on tiptoe, craning her neck as her gaze swept the broad expanse of sand. Beneath her feet the ground vibrated as each wave rolled in to pound the beach in a welter of foam and spray.

'Hey! Miss!' the driver called. 'Shall I take you back now?'

Laura glanced at him over her shoulder. 'No, not yet. I...I can't go yet.' He was probably here and she just couldn't see him. The beach was long and the lights did not shine very far over the sand. *He had to be here.*

'Sorry, miss, but I can't hang about. The wife's got my supper waiting. You were my last fare tonight. I only picked you up because it looked like an emergency.' The driver's tone made it clear he thought he'd been stopped under false pretences. 'I've been on since eight this morning.'

'I'm sorry.' Laura searched her purse for the fare, adding a generous tip.

'You're not staying here on your own?' The driver sounded concerned.

'I'll be quite all right,' Laura assured him. 'I . . . I'm meeting someone.'

His expression made it clear he thought it a very odd choice of rendezvous, but the pull of his supper overcame his concern. 'That's all right then.' Absolved of responsibility, he revved up and, with a final nod, drove away.

Laura shivered and looked about her. The snack-bars were shuttered and locked, and there wasn't a person in sight. The tall street lights cast a pale eerie glow over the sand-strewn road and upper part of the beach.

After a moment, Laura slipped her shoes off and stepped down on to the soft, cool sand. It felt marvellous after the hardness of the city's streets. She started down towards the water's edge.

Despite the wind, the air was mild, and there was a freshness in it that cleared her head as it moulded her dress to her body.

She walked along the beach, just out of reach of the rushing waves, peering through the darkness, straining her eyes. He *must* be here. *He had to be.* But the beach was deserted.

She turned back, retracing her steps, and recalled the moment Brent had held her for the first time and they had danced. Two sets of footprints had marked the wet sand. Now there was only one and the hungry sea was reaching for those.

Laura's eyes filled and hot tears trickled down her cheeks. Why had it all gone so terribly wrong? Why had Gavin and Cheryl turned up *now*? And why, oh *why*, wouldn't Jeremy just leave her alone?

Seeing the four of them at the bar drinking champagne, it must have looked to Brent as though they were having a party.

She would never forget the look of devastation on his face. This had been her last desperate hope.

She brushed her hand across her wet eyes and tried to choke back the sobs. What was the point of weeping? It didn't ease the hurt and it wouldn't bring him back.

If he didn't want to listen, if he wouldn't let her explain the whole unfortunate misunderstanding, there was nothing more she could do.

But it hurt so much that he had judged her without even a hearing. He couldn't have cared as much as she thought. She had reflected her growing feelings on to him, imagined he was becoming as involved as she was. Yet, hadn't he said as much? That he had sensed something between them from that first moment? Then *why* hadn't he answered her calls? Why hadn't he waited?

She stopped and looked out to sea. The salt wind dried her tears and streamed her hair back from her hot face. She was so tired. It was time to go back.

She turned to start up the beach and froze with a gasp. Half-way between her and the road, a still figure was silhouetted against the glow of the street light.

There was a buzzing in her head and for one terrible moment she thought she really would faint. She took a step forwards. 'Brent?' Her whisper was borne away on the wind.

'Are you all right?' The figure moved towards her. She stopped dead, rigid with fear.

'Who are you?'

'Police, miss. We had a call from a taxi driver who was a bit concerned about a fare he'd picked up. He said the young lady seemed rather distraught, and wanted to be left on the beach. Alone. In the dark.' The policeman's measured tone held no censure, just concern. 'Perhaps you'd like to go home now, miss. We can give you a lift.'

Laura sighed, a deep, shuddering breath. 'Thank you. I...I'd appreciate it.'

A second policeman sat in the driving-seat and, while he guided the car back towards the city centre, Laura heard the first one quietly asking his control to check with the Holiday Inn that she was registered there.

The car drew up a little way from the hotel and the first officer turned in his seat. 'All right now, miss?'

Laura opened the door. 'Yes. Thank you.' She hesitated. 'I wonder would you do something for me? You probably know all the taxi drivers well. When you see the one who called, would you thank him, from me? He needn't have been worried, I wasn't going to—I really had expected to meet someone there but...' her throat was suddenly stiff with tears, 'he...he didn't turn up.' She climbed out quickly. 'Thank you for the lift. Goodnight.'

'Goodnight, miss. Er, miss?'

Laura glanced back as the policeman wound his window down a little further.

'I'd get yourself another bloke.' With a final salute, he motioned the driver forward and they drove off.

CHAPTER TEN

As she reached her door, Laura heard the phone ringing. In her haste she fumbled the key and almost dropped it.

Kicking the door shut and losing one shoe in the process, she raced across the room and, as she dived forward to pick up the phone, it stopped ringing.

She stared at it, her body shaking with the force of her heart-beat. *One last time*. Snatching up the receiver, clasping it in trembling hands, she asked for Brent's room.

'What is this game you are playing, hide and seek?' Inez sounded curious. 'Four times this evening he has rung for you and you do not answer. Now you ask for him!'

'What?' *He had been ringing her?* 'What are you doing there?' Laura blurted in surprise, easing off her remaining shoe.

'The holiday season is starting so sometimes I do late shift,' Inez explained, 'and as Jaime has the evening off, we are one short. Now, I put you through. Goodnight, Laura. I hope...I hope all is well.'

'Goodnight Inez.' The line went dead as Inez switched off her own connection. Then Laura heard the buzz as it rang in Brent's room. *He had tried to reach her*.

It was answered on the second ring. 'Yes?' Brent demanded curtly.

Laura clutched the receiver. 'Brent? I——'

'Laura?' His voice was sharp.

'Yes, I——'

'Where are you calling from?' He rapped the words out.

'I'm in my room. I've just got back. Were you——'

'Stay there. I'm coming over.'

'Wait, Brent. I——'

The line went dead. Laura replaced the receiver. *He wanted to see her.* So why hadn't he answered when she phoned him? She replaced the receiver and started to run one hand through her hair, wincing as her fingers encountered the tangles.

She hurried to the mirror and was aghast at what she saw. She had no lipstick left. Her hair, wildly tumbled by the wind, looked as though a flock of birds had been nesting in it, and her cheeks were smudged with mascara where she had wiped her tears with the heel of her hand. She looked nearer fifteen than twenty-five.

Seizing a comb she tried to restore some order, but the knots almost defeated her. Maybe if she could just wash her face and repair her make-up—a sharp rapping on the door stopped her half-way to the bathroom.

Taking a deep breath, she put her head close to the door. 'Who is it?'

Brent's deep voice came clearly through the wood. 'How many people are you expecting?'

Laura opened the door. 'None,' she answered coolly. 'I wasn't *expecting* you.'

They stared at one another, each enclosed in their own hurt and anger.

'May I come in?' Brent was icily polite.

Laura stepped back, opening the door wide enough for him to enter, knowing that, by the time he left, the situation between them would have been finally resolved, *one way or the other.*

As she closed the door, he pushed his hands into his pockets, and simply stood, waiting. He had discarded the jacket and tie she had glimpsed earlier in the bar, and wore only navy slacks and a pale blue shirt open at the neck, with the sleeves rolled half-way up his forearms.

Acutely aware of her own dishevelment, Laura's hand crept up to her face. 'I—I was just going to tidy up.' Her cheeks flamed under his raking gaze.

'You've been crying,' he said softly in a tone that combined accusation with surprise and concern.

'Ten out of ten for observation.' Her chin thrust defiantly and she glared at him.

He seized her shoulders. 'Don't take that tone with me. Why didn't you answer when I phoned?'

'Why didn't *you*?' she shot back.

He looked startled. 'You called me?'

'Yes, three times.' She hadn't meant to tell him that. It slipped out. *Where was her pride?* To hell with pride. What happened now was of far too much importance to allow foolish ideas about pride to get in the way.

'Answer my question,' he demanded, his eyes diamond-hard and glittering.

'I wasn't here.'

'Where were you?'

'Out.' She caught her breath as his grip tightened.

'With Grainger?'

'*No!* I left Jeremy at the bar. I was alone. I went looking for you. I wanted to explain——'

His laugh was a single, explosive bark, and Laura quailed at its bitterness and contempt. 'How interesting.' His features were granite-hard and his voice flayed her. 'Explain what? That you had known all along your brother was marrying my ex-fiancée? I see now why you were so reluctant to talk about him.'

She should have realised he would notice.

Laura exploded. 'I did not *know*. It was only a guess. I'd had a letter from Gavin in which he mentioned the girl he was marrying——'

'You expect me to believe that?' Brent cut in tersely. 'This brother you're so close to, who writes and phones with such commendable regularity, only *mentioned* the girl he planned to marry?'

Laura shook her head helplessly. 'It's true. I was surprised myself. He told me only enough to make me wonder if it *could* be the same girl, *of course* I didn't say anything to you. I wasn't *sure*. And, in any case, it was none of my business.'

'You might at least have warned me they were coming,' he threw at her.

'I didn't even know until I met Gavin in the foyer,' she hurled back. 'He said in his letter that they hoped to call, but he didn't say when. I thought it would be weeks before they got here.' Her voice fell. 'You would have gone by then.'

'And you would have kept quiet about the whole thing?' He sounded angrier than ever.

'What was I supposed to do?' she cried. 'I was trying not to cause any unnecessary problems by saying something that might not have been true. Why does it matter to you anyway?' Laura couldn't prevent some of her anguish spilling over. 'Why shouldn't Cheryl have found happiness with someone else? *You* were the one who decided a fiancé wasn't enough, you had to have an affair as well.'

She watched him visibly pale. He looked totally shocked. 'Who told you that?'

She bent her head. 'What does it matter?' she murmured.

'It matters all right,' he grated, shaking her, 'because it isn't true.'

Laura's head flew up. 'But . . . according to the papers you and Cheryl split up because of someone else.'

Brent's eyes narrowed and his mouth twisted in a cynical smile. 'That's right, we did. Only everyone jumped to the wrong conclusion. It was not *me* who was having the affair, it was *Cheryl*. And do you know *who* she was involved with? *Your brother.*' He released her so abruptly she staggered backwards.

Laura was deeply shaken. 'Oh, *no*.' Unconsciously she rubbed her arms where his fingers had dug into them as her thoughts raced. She did not doubt he was telling the truth. Even had she not known that lying was anathema to him, his bitter anger would have been evidence enough. Yet it was so hard to believe.

Suddenly she understood so many things that had puzzled her, his initial reaction to her, not because she was Gavin's sister, he hadn't known that then, but the fact that he was immediately attracted to her after having been so badly hurt, his suspicion of the growing feeling between them, and his determination to remain uncommitted. It made his behaviour, and especially the incident on the beach, so much easier to understand.

'Oh *yes*,' he muttered savagely. 'And I didn't have the faintest idea what was going on behind my back. God, what a fool.'

'No,' Laura shook her head. 'Not a fool, not you.'

He folded himself into the chair by Laura's desk and clasped his head in his hands. She felt pity welling up inside her. No wonder he had been shocked to see Cheryl and to learn that Gavin was her brother. And yet the couple seemed so genuinely happy. They were clearly devoted to one another, to the extent that Cheryl showed small but distinct signs of jealousy at having to share Gavin even with his own sister.

Laura perched on the end of the bed. She had been too badly mauled herself, had suffered too much over the last few hours simply to brush it all aside. She was not ready simply to forgive and forget, there were still too many questions unanswered.

'Brent?'

He raised his head. He looked tired and drawn.

'I know my brother. He wouldn't poach on another man's territory. Cheryl's the first girl he's ever been seriously involved with. He's besotted with her. I only met her today so obviously I can't know her well, but she doesn't seem the sort of girl to play around.' Laura chose her words carefully, feeling her way. She didn't want to rub salt in the wound, but she needed to know the truth. 'Something...couldn't have been right between you and Cheryl. Why did she turn to Gavin? There must have been a reason.'

Brent's face had darkened as she spoke. He glowered at her now and mentally she cringed, waiting for the explosion. He sprang out of the chair and began to pace the room, rubbing the back of his neck. After a long pause, he shot her a sideways glance then threw up both hands in a gesture of surrender.

'You're right,' he admitted. 'I suppose I didn't see it then, but time and...' his expression softened '...other things have given me a rather different view.'

Laura's heart quickened.

Brent went on, 'I guess the root of the problem was that she and I were too much alike. You may not have seen enough of Cheryl yet to realise that she is extremely ambitious.'

Laura nodded. 'She doesn't exactly make a secret of it. But surely that's no bad thing? She's very talented.'

'I'm not disputing that,' Brent said, 'in fact I admire her. She deserves success, she has certainly worked for it. But I was under a lot of pressure as well. I had more commissions and assignments than I could cope with.' He shrugged and, with his hands in his pockets, leaned against the wall and gazed out of the window into the light-sprinkled darkness. 'I suppose,' he spoke hesitantly, confronting, for the first time, the real reason for the break-up, 'when it came to the crunch, we were both too selfish. We each put our own career first. Both of us wanted backing and emotional support, but neither had time to give it.'

Laura recalled her brother's face alight with love and excitement as he outlined the future he and Cheryl had mapped out. He had cheerfully abandoned his own career to channel his financial expertise into building up hers. As for Cheryl, Laura sensed that though the girl's artistic flair meant she would always be something of a free spirit, she would also be totally loyal to Gavin in return for his loving support and business acumen. They would make an unsinkable partnership.

A wry smile lifted the corners of Brent's mouth. 'I see now we were quite wrong for each other. Neither of us was prepared to compromise.' He turned to face her. 'Odd isn't it, that I should now be seriously considering cutting back on the amount of travelling I do. I don't *need* to work at this pressure. It's just a habit.'

For a fleeting instant, Laura had the impression he was trying to tell her something without actually putting it into words. But everything was still too precarious for her to risk making an assumption, so she dismissed the idea.

'I've reached the same conclusion myself, about *my* work, I mean,' Laura said quietly. 'In fact, I've decided to do something about it. Tonight was the last straw.' She looked up at him. 'I'm resigning from Phoenix.'

He tensed. 'You're *what*?'

'I'm leaving the company.'

His features tightened. 'You can't, you gave your word to Dennis.'

'Don't you think I've thought of that?' she cried, and looked down at her clasped hands. 'I just can't go on— I don't want further promotion and life is too short to waste it in a job I'm no longer happy with.'

'You're running away,' he accused.

'I'd be far more secure, financially, if I stayed put,' she countered.

Brent sat down beside her on the foot of the bed and she wondered with sudden desperation how she would hide the effect his nearness had on her.

'It's Grainger, isn't it?' He caught her chin, forcing her to look at him. 'Isn't it?' he repeated.

Her skin prickled as though charged with electricity. 'Partly,' she allowed, 'but he's not the only reason.'

'Laura, listen.' Brent released her chin and covered her hand with his own. 'I spent most of this evening down at the Port Office with Sam Lincoln.'

Her head came up and she stiffened. '*Terrific*. If you had spared a moment to tell me of your plans instead of walking out in a huff, I'd have been spared a lot of grief, not to mention an encounter with the police!'

His whole body jerked round, his face livid with concern. '*What?* What happened? How did you get involved with the police, for God's sake?'

'It was nothing,' she said quickly, wishing she had held her tongue. That had been a cheap gibe. 'Just a misunderstanding. I took a taxi out to the beach and the driver thought... well, he was worried and called the police who gave me a lift back to the hotel.' She shrugged and tried to smile. 'That was all there was to it. A lot of fuss about nothing.'

Brent slid his arm around her shoulders and drew her close against him.

She kept her eyes lowered. When he touched her, held her, she felt incredibly, vibrantly *alive*.

'Why the beach, Laura?' His voice was low, perplexed.

'Because I'd tried everywhere else I could think of,' she blurted. 'That was my last hope.' She lifted one shoulder, withdrawing a little. 'Just a stupid whim.'

'You went there alone? In the dark? With a near-gale blowing?' His voice rose as anger at the risk she had taken overcame his attempt to understand. 'Do you realise what might——?'

'Nothing happened,' she broke in. 'You weren't there. I came home. End of story.' She tried to pull free and get up, but he held her fast.

'Damn it, Laura.' Roughly he turned her face to his, frowning deeply. 'Of all the foolish—you *idiot*, I——' With a brief groan he covered her mouth with his own. He pushed her backwards and they sprawled on to the pink coverlet. His body half covered hers and his warm weight took her breath away.

His kiss was hard, demanding, a kiss of anger and of fear at what might have befallen her. It contained all the stormy emotions that had raged between them. Then, as the tempest passed, it asked forgiveness and offered comfort.

Brent raised himself on one elbow, gently smoothing her hair back from her forehead as they both fought to steady their breathing.

Laura looked up at him. 'Why, Brent? Why didn't you wait? Why did you go to Sam?'

A muscle jumped in his jaw. 'Because if I'd come into the bar, I'd have smashed Grainger to a pulp. Seeing him there—you looked so terribly unhappy. Cheryl turning up here with her lover——'

'Husband,' Laura corrected softly.

'All right, husband,' he growled, 'gave me a shock and, I must admit, it hurt to think you'd deliberately kept it secret from me.' As she drew breath to protest he placed his fingertips over her mouth. 'I accept it wasn't quite as I thought.' His voice hardened. 'But I've watched your confidence ebb since Grainger turned up. I've a pretty good idea of how hard you've had to work to get where you are. Dennis thinks the world of you, and with good reason. And Grainger is trying, just as he did before, to sabotage your working relationships and demolish your confidence.'

'No,' Laura began, unwilling to admit it openly.

'Stop kidding yourself.' He was impatient. 'Grainger is out to destroy you.' His voice was cold and implacable. 'I am not prepared to let that happen.'

'Are you absolutely sure about Jeremy?' she whispered in horror, even as Brent's determined protection of her made her dizzy with joy.

'Ask Sam Lincoln. He was the first to be subjected to Grainger's creeping poison to ease you out of favour and himself in. Sam and I phoned the heads of the companies Grainger has visited since his arrival here. He hadn't wasted any time, there were quite a few. They are all pretty astute, but he's such a tricky bastard they hadn't realised what he was up to. With just a few veiled insinuations about previous poor management and the overburdening of unqualified assistant staff he made himself look like the company's saviour.' Brent's features were taut with disgust.

'Next I used a few of my contacts in London and Rotterdam to dig up some information about Grainger's business record. Laura, I can not only get him fired, I can also prevent him ever getting another job connected with port development.'

Laura wriggled free and sat up. 'Brent, you can't. You can't use it. I'm not trying to protect Jeremy. God knows, I detest him. But a scandal like that would cripple Phoenix. Dennis put everything he had into this project, even his health. He's only just recovering from major surgery. What do you think the publicity would do to him?'

Brent remained quite still, leaning on one elbow. 'Laura, if Grainger stays, he'll damage the company beyond repair. There'll be nothing for Dennis to come back to if he isn't stopped.'

Unable to remain still a moment longer, she slid off the bed and went to the window. Opening it, she breathed in the cool night air, and listened to the rustle and cry of the masses of birds roosting on the slopes of the upper rock. She turned to face Brent. 'I can't destroy him. That would make me as bad as he is.'

Swiftly, Brent got off the bed, and as he came towards her Laura felt every nerve begin to tighten.

'Tell me the truth, Laura, would you still want to resign if Grainger were no longer here?'

She swallowed. 'Yes. But not until the project is finished.'

Suddenly he smiled. 'I had to be sure. I've something else to tell you. I made another call. To the chairman of the board of the Phoenix Group.'

Laura's eyes widened. 'You *what*?' she gasped.

His eyes held a strange light as he rested his hands on her shoulders. 'I told him exactly what I had found out about Grainger, and the threat to the project if he stayed. But I gave my word that I'd use none of it provided Grainger was recalled from Gibraltar within forty-eight hours.'

Laura gaped at him, speechless.

'It seemed mere common sense that, as you knew more about the job than anyone else, and were more capable, you should be made Project Manager. He agreed to everything.' A smile of satisfaction flickered at the corners of Brent's mouth. 'An eminently practical man. No doubt he'll find a desk job somewhere in the group for Grainger. Well?' He shook her very gently. 'No comment?'

'I—I—thank you, Brent,' she said softly, 'no one but you could have done it. I can't tell you how grateful I am.'

'We'll come to that in a minute.' He took his hands from her shoulders and immediately Laura missed their warm weight, but he caught her around the waist, and, linking his fingers behind her, swung her to and fro.

'Where had you planned to go when you left here?'

She could feel the play of muscle beneath her fingers where they lay on his arms. 'Back to England.'

'To do what?'

She steeled herself for his reactions. She would know then. If he laughed... 'Write.'

His dark brows rose and he was suddenly still, his gaze intent. 'Why?' he asked quietly.

'Because it's something I really enjoy doing,' she replied with total honesty. 'And I'd like to develop whatever talent I may have for it.' She grinned impishly. 'I'm not a complete beginner you know. Two articles in *Wildlife* isn't a bad start.'

He grasped her hands. Raising them to his lips, he kissed each one in turn, then held them against his chest, forcing her to come nearer.

'I'm planning some changes too.' His voice was deep, vibrant. 'I'm going to cut back on the travelling. It's time to put down roots. A house can never be a real home unless one spends time in it. And with five acres...'

'And a beech wood,' Laura added softly, recalling the vivid picture he had painted with his description. Then realising she had spoken aloud, she flushed to the roots of her hair. She peeped up at Brent. His smile was a mixture of triumph and tenderness, and what she saw in his eyes made her breath catch in her throat.

'And a beech wood,' he echoed, 'a place that needs a lot of time, and a lot of love, and children.' He paused. 'Laura, I'm committed to the Hong Kong trip just as you are committed here, but when I get back, I...I think we should get married.'

Happiness filled Laura with a golden radiance. 'Why?' she enquired innocently.

He looked stunned. '*Why?* Because...because...' His frown cleared as he realised she was teasing. 'Because I love you.' His voice was as potent as a caress and a delicious shiver feathered down her spine.

'And I love you,' she told him, overjoyed to be able to say the words at last. Looking into his eyes she saw them blaze with delight, relief and desire.

'Then we'll get married as soon as I get back.'

She shook her head. 'No.'

His features darkened menacingly. 'Don't play games with me, Laura,' he warned.

Pulling her hands free, she placed them on either side of his face, and feeling the warmth mounting in her cheeks she whispered, 'It's an awful long time to wait. Couldn't we get married before you go?'

He put his arms around her. 'Now why didn't I think of that?'

Running her fingers through his hair, she shook her head. 'Sometimes you're awfully slow.'

He kissed her, a long lingering kiss that fanned the flames until they were both breathless. Then, using only one arm, he reached up and pulled the curtains across.

'We'll honeymoon in Tangier,' he murmured, and kissed her again.

'We won't have very long,' Laura sighed, savouring him with all her senses.

'We'll have a lifetime,' he promised. There was silence then, 'How grateful did you say you were?'

Laura's exultant laughter floated out on to the warm night air.

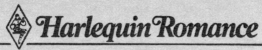 **Harlequin Romance**

Coming Next Month

2929 LOSING BATTLE Kerry Allyne
Adair has good reasons for the way she dresses and looks. She's not
about to change because of arrogant Thane Callahan. After all, he's
seemingly no different than the men who'd caused her bitter lack
of trust.

2930 BLACK SHEEP Susan Fox
Willa Ross returns to her hometown of Cascade, Wyoming, only to
discover she's still drawn to the man she'd been love-struck with as
a teenager—and he still blames her for the accident that caused his
sister's death.

2931 RIDER OF THE HILLS Miriam MacGregor
Janie's only chance of getting an interview with New Zealand's
famous polo player, Lance Winter, is to temporarily replace his
injured trainer. Once there, however, she finds her prime concern
is what Lance will think of her deception!

2932 HEART'S TREASURE Annabel Murray
Jacques Fresnay's involvement in the Peruvian expedition is a
surprise to Rylla. Equally surprising is that he seems to be genuinely
kind, though he'd ridiculed her father's work. Should she abide by
family loyalty, or give in to Jacques's charm?

2933 THE COURSE OF TRUE LOVE Betty Neels
Claribel's current attentive male friends begin to lack interest when
consulting surgeon Marc van Borsele arrogantly breaks into her life.
Suddenly he's giving her a lift in his Rolls, appearing at work in the
London Hospital, standing on her doorstep. Why? Claribel
wondered.

2934 SNOWY RIVER MAN Valerie Parv
Gemma's family had been hounded from their hometown because
everyone thought her father a thief. Now Gemma wants to clear his
name. But the only guide available to help her search for his body
and the missing money is Robb Weatherill, whose father had been
loudest in denouncing hers....

Available in September wherever paperback books are sold,
or through Harlequin Reader Service:

In the U.S.	In Canada
901 Fuhrmann Blvd.	P.O. Box 603
P.O. Box 1397	Fort Erie, Ontario
Buffalo, N.Y. 14240-1397	L2A 5X3

Temptation™

TEMPTATION WILL BE
EVEN HARDER TO RESIST...

In September, Temptation is presenting a sophisticated new face to the world. A fresh look that truly brings Harlequin's most intimate romances into focus.

What's more, all-time favorite authors Barbara Delinsky, Rita Clay Estrada, Jayne Ann Krentz and Vicki Lewis Thompson will join forces to help us celebrate. The result? A very special quartet of Temptations...

- Four striking covers
- Four stellar authors
- Four sensual love stories
- Four variations on one spellbinding theme

All in one great month! Give in to Temptation in September.

TDESIGN-1

Harlequin Intrigue

Two exciting new stories each month.

Each title mixes a contemporary, sophisticated romance with the surprising twists and turns of a puzzler...romance with "something more."

Because romance can be quite an adventure.

Romance, Suspense and Adventure